W9-DCJ-491

Miles To Go

"If you don't like the way I drive—" Jessica Pace stopped talking as she cut the wheel left pulling the moving car off the shoulder, the trailer swaying behind the car again. "—Then you can—" Frost turned and looked at her, saw her looking at him, then saw that they were crossing over into the oncoming lanes.

"All right—stop the car. Now!"

She did, and Frost almost smacked his head against the dashboard.

He ran around to the front of the car, thinking better of it—what if she hadn't set the parking brake? Frost adjusted the seat, released the emergency brake, and started to move the selector into drive.

"Sucker," she snapped. "I not only went through CIA's counterterrorist driving course, I went through the same thing for the KGB—and I taught regular driving when I was working my way through graduate school. It supported my habit out at the drag strip. I used to race class—"

"Ohh." Frost lit a cigarette and rolled down the window, staring into the rear-view mirror. It was, he decided, going to be a long drive to Phoenix. . . .

THE SURVIVALIST SERIES
by Jerry Ahern

THE SURVIVALIST #1: TOTAL WAR (768, $2.25)
The first in the shocking series that follows the unrelenting search for
ex-CIA covert operations officer John Thomas Rourke to locate his
missing family—after the button is pressed, the missiles launched and
the multimegaton bombs unleashed . . .

THE SURVIVALIST #2:
THE NIGHTMARE BEGINS (810, $2.50)
After WW III, the United States is just a memory. But ex-CIA covert
operations officer Rourke hasn't forgotten his family. While hiding
from the Soviet occupation forces, he adheres to his search!

THE SURVIVALIST #3: THE QUEST (851, $2.50)
Not even a deadly game of intrigue within the Soviet High Command,
the formation of the American "resistance" and a highly placed
traitor in the new U.S. government can deter Rourke from continuing
his desperate search for his family.

THE SURVIVALIST #4: THE DOOMSAYER (893, $2.50)
The most massive earthquake in history is only hours away, and
Communist-Cuban troops, Soviet-Cuban rivalry, and a traitor in the
inner circle of U.S.II block Rourke's path. But he must go on—he is
THE SURVIVALIST.

*Available wherever paperbacks are sold, or order direct from the
Publisher. Send cover price plus 50¢ per copy for mailing and han-
dling to Zebra Books, 475 Park Avenue South, New York, N.Y. 10016.
DO NOT SEND CASH.*

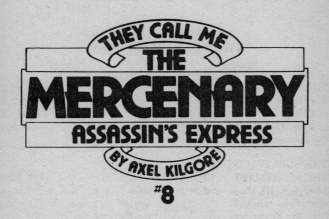

THEY CALL ME

THE

MERCENARY

ASSASSIN'S EXPRESS

BY AXEL KILGORE

#8

ZEBRA BOOKS
KENSINGTON PUBLISHING CORP.

ZEBRA BOOKS

are published by

KENSINGTON PUBLISHING CORP.
475 Park Avenue South
New York, N.Y. 10016

Copyright © 1982 by Axel Kilgore

All rights reserved. No part of this book may be
reproduced in any form or by any means without the
prior written consent of the Publisher, excepting brief
quotes used in reviews.

Printed in the United States of America

Any resemblance to persons, governments, businesses or governmental entities living, dead, or operating or having operated, is purely coincidental.

Chapter One

"Go ahead—buy it. That's all you talk about—or used to. 'When I get some money, maybe I'll buy a Rolex.' So buy it, You can afford to marry me—so buy yourself the wrist watch—go on!"

Frost turned and looked at Bess, her green eyes, the blond hair that fell past her shoulders now. "Trying to civilize me?"

"No—never, Frost." She smiled, the soft alto of her voice something that Frost felt he'd never tire of.

"All right," Frost said, turning back to the woman behind the jewelry counter. "I'll take it."

"The Rolex Seadweller, sir?" The girl had blue eyes, reddish hair, and the classic English ruddy-cheeked look—she was about twenty-five.

"Yeah," he told the woman. "That and the ring—will you take a traveler's check?"

"Of course sir—I'll need some identification though."

Frost nodded as the woman busied herself behind the counter. He turned back toward Bess, but couldn't see her; then he spotted her on the far side of the store. Telling the clerk he'd be back in a moment, Frost worked his way through the maze of counters and department-store shoppers, finally getting up beside Bess. "You talk about me being dull." He laughed; Bess turned, startled, then smiled. "What are you doing—looking at luggage!"

"I've lived in London a long time—a lot to pack," she said absently.

"You happy?"

She looked at him, the corners of her mouth slightly crinkled in a smile. "What do you think? I mean, I really didn't think you'd do it, Frost. You're not the marrying kind."

"Yeah, well . . ." Frost shrugged.

"I've gotta tell you—I just can't—"

"Can't what?" Frost asked her.

"Well, my folks—they wanted to get a wedding cake for us. My mother and I talked. She knew you had one eye. So—well, you know the little people they put on top of the wedding cake? Well, she had this friend of hers—he's an artist. Well, they fixed the little man on the wedding cake to have an eye patch. You don't mind?"

8

"You've gotta be kiddin' me."

"No—you mind, don't you. I mean—"

Frost took her in his arms.

"The people in the store—"

"The hell with 'em," Frost said with an air of finality, kissing her not too lightly on the mouth.

Gently, she pushed away from him, then leaned up quickly and kissed his cheek. "Are you going to be like this after we're married twenty-five years, Frost?"

"Uh-huh," he said, gently running his hand across her shoulders, holding her.

"I was afraid of that." She laughed.

Frost and Bess started back across the store, toward the jewelry counter. Frost decided then it was impossible for a woman to take more than three uninterrupted steps in a department store. She stopped to look at almost everything they passed. A shiver ran up his spine as she looked at some peculiar clothing, because after a moment, he realized it was for children. Frost tried to imagine somebody calling him Daddy and shook his head in disbelief at the thought, but then smiled. Maybe it wouldn't be so bad—not with Bess, he decided. They reached the jewelry counter again, the woman having had the Rolex's band adjusted. Frost tried it on. "Looks good, Frost—goes with the sixty-five-dollar shoes," Bess told him.

"Terrific." Frost wrote the traveler's checks, commenting to Bess and the clerk he'd have to get more of them. He pocketed his old watch, along with the sales slip for the new one. Then the girl brought the ring. Frost opened the box, letting Bess see the engagement ring for the first time. "You like it?"

"Where'd you find a setting like this?" She took the ring from the small velvet box and turned it over in her hands. The diamond was set in a heavy yellow-gold ring, the band itself having the appearance of chains wrapped tightly around one another, almost braided. Around the stone itself was the head of a roaring, open-mouthed tiger, as though the diamond were set in the jaws.

"You don't like it," Frost said, taking it from her and looking at it a moment.

"Well—I've never seen anything like it. I do like it—it's beautiful" she told him. "Where did you find—"

Frost looked at her eyes, then said, "Years back, in Vietnam. There was this old man, caught under some building rubble after a V.C. mortar attack. Nobody wanted to bother getting him out—they said he was dying anyway. Well—you know—"

"I know you," she said, her voice strangely soft, warm-sounding to him.

"Well, I dug him out—you know. He spoke a little English, I spoke a little Vietnamese. We talked. He was dying, but at least in the sunlight. He gave me the ring. He'd sold the stone to get food for his grandchildren once, but he'd kept the ring—been in his family, his grandmother had told him, for a long time. Well, his grandchildren had died—no one left. He wanted to give it to me. I told him I could bury it with him, but he said he'd rather I kept it. I told him I would—and I have. I had it sized down to fit you," Frost concluded, slipping the ring on the third finger of her left hand. "You happy with it?"

"Ohh, Frost." She leaned up, hugging her arms around his neck, then kissed him quickly on the mouth. "Yes—I love you," she whispered.

This time Frost turned around, noticing some old women staring at them. He wanted to thumb his nose at them, but didn't. He looked back at Bess and there were tears in her eyes. "What's the matter?"

"Nothing—nothing, Frost. You finish here—I'm going to the ladies' room a minute." She leaned up, kissed his cheek, and turning on her high heels, started into the crowd.

"If you don't mind my saying so," the young woman clerk began, "congratulations."

Frost smiled at her. "Thank you." He nodded, taking the empty ring box and the receipt. He looked at his wrist, staring at the watch. "A Rolex," he muttered, smiling. He decided to stay near the jewelry counter while he waited for Bess. As a little boy, once he'd gotten lost in a department store—only for five minutes—but ever since, the places had given him the creeps.

There was a counter with electronic games not far away. Frost mentally and physically shrugged, walking toward it.

There was a loud roaring noise and something seemed to slap at him from behind. The one-eyed man fell forward into the glass case, shoving his hands up to protect his face; then darkness washed over him. . . .

Frost opened his eye, muttering something, then

looked at the man sitting next to him. "Sorry—fell asleep," he rasped, then turned and stared out the window, yawning. It was a clear day; fields checkerboarded under the aircraft were visible in alternating patches of light and shadow, once the shadow of the aircraft itself had cleared the ground below.

Frost lit a cigarette. "Bess," he whispered, still staring out.

The explosion in the London department store had almost vaporized the section of the first floor where Bess had been—the grave in the cemetery in northwest suburban Chicago near where her parents lived was empty; no remains were to be found. In all, including Bess, eleven people had been killed in the terrorist bombing. Frost himself had been knocked unconscious by the shock wave and had suffered minor cuts and bruises. Sixty-seven other people had been injured, to varying degrees.

Released from the hospital emergency room later that same day, Frost had gone back to the department-store site, the area cordoned off by police. He had simply stood there. Finally, around one in the morning, a police sergeant had walked up to him, and asked him why he stood there. Then Frost had started to talk. Death carried with it one curious human characteristic, Frost reflected, stubbing out his Camel and staring at the fringe of cloud cover starting beneath the aircraft. You started to talk, even to a perfect stranger; and because you had to talk—maybe to keep your sanity—you told the stranger things you wouldn't usually admit even to yourself. The sergeant was on a break and Frost and the man had gone into a still-open pub, the officer

12

having coffee because he was technically on duty, Frost just having a beer—Frost knew himself well enough from the old days to realize that if he had begun to drink hard liquor he wouldn't have stopped. Frost had told the sergeant what kind of a girl Bess had been, about their marriage plans, about how they'd met—even about the thing Bess had told him concerning the couple on top of the wedding cake, having the eye patch painted in there.

Frost had still been wrestling with the idea of switching from beer to the hard stuff when the sergeant, tired-sounding, had begun to talk. Frost closed his eye, listening to the drone of the aircraft engines, remembering what the sergeant had said then. "I seen a lot of these bombings, I have. When I was just a bloke, I remember the Gerries bombing us, the way I'd 'ear some voice crying out of the rubble. I'd ask my mum why the Gerries dropped their bombs and made people suffer that way. My mum—God rest 'er soul—she told me, ' 'arry—if you ever start t' understand why, look out fer yerself,' she said. I didn't understand 'er then, but I do now. There ain't no way to understand the likes of them terrorist bombers—because they ain't human. You understand 'em, you gotta be like 'em. I can read it in that one eye of yours, I can. You don't understand why them terrorists'd bomb a department store, kill innocents—and it's to your credit that you don't."

Frost wondered if *they* understood—the terrorists? He had dutifully called Bess's parents, faintly thought they somehow blamed him. Frost had started wondering if violence were just naturallyl at-

13

tracted to him.

Frost had spent the next three weeks haunting New Scotland Yard, making the rounds of the pubs the I.R.A. people were rumored to frequent. And the whole thing had made him feel impotent—nothing had come of it. The London Police weren't even able to pinpoint which cell of the I.R.A. might have been responsible, if indeed it were the I.R.A. at all. Frost had thought of going to Ireland—northern or southern. Just to find somebody in the I.R.A. and kill for retribution—but he'd remembered the police sergeant then as he did now. Just finding some man who belonged to the I.R.A. and gratuitously killing was the sort of thing a terrorist would do.

Frost had feelers out with everyone he knew who kept tabs on the terrorist movement—the Egyptian agent, Sharif Abdusalem; his old contacts in the Israeli Mossad; his friend, Nifkawitz, from the CIA. All he wanted was a lead, just one. Then Frost smiled, the cloud cover through his window complete; he would find out just who it was he had to kill, who had planted the bomb in the department store—who had killed Bess. Frost closed his eye and tried to control his breathing—it was either that or cry. . . .

Frost stood in the aircraft washroom, splashing cold water on his face; then stared at himself in the mirror, his eye patch removed. The scar was ugly—it always had been. It had never bothered Bess, though. Frost splashed more water on his face, lamenting the fact then that men weren't supposed to scream. After putting more water on his face, then drying it with brown paper towels, he put the eye patch back into position.

The one-eyed man stared at himself in the mirror. Was the hatred he had for the unknown bomber because of what the terrorist had done to Bess, or because of what Bess's death had done to him? Frost looked at the Rolex watch on his wrist—at least Bess had died wearing the ring he'd given her. He thought about the dying old man who had given him the ring in Vietnam—was it bad luck?

Frost looked angrily toward the door—someone was knocking on it. He shook his head, opened the door, and looked into the eyes of a stewardess. "Are you all right, sir?"

"What? Oh, yeah—just a little airsick."

"I can give you—"

"No," Frost said, smiling at her. "I'm fine now," he lied, then walked past her and down the aisle toward his seat. He crawled over the man on the aisle and sat down, staring at the clouds again. He'd returned to the United States from London almost a week earlier, dropped down in Florida and visited his old friend Lou Wilson, then bummed around Miami for a while. He'd had the early model Interdynamics KG-9 retrofitted with the sling swivels now standard on these guns, had found a range, and had eaten up several boxes of 9-mm 115-grain JHPs in both the Metalifed Browning and the KG-9. He hadn't fired a gun in more than a month and his first few targets had reflected that.

Finally, Frost had gotten up the nerve to fly back to Chicago and return to his apartment in South

Bend—he'd told Bess about the place, promising he wouldn't make her live there. Going to the barren rooms with the 1969-vintage black-and-white television, the few chairs, the picture of Bess on the dresser—he'd gone out to get a drink. There had been whiskey in the cupboard, but he'd gone out anyway. If you paid for the stuff by the glassful, somehow you drank it more slowly—at least that had always worked for him.

At the bar, he had bumped into Claudia Minish, Andrew Deacon's secretary at Diablo Protective Services. Claudia had never been fond of him, Frost had thought, but seeing him she had run up to him, thrown her arms around his neck, hugged him, and acted generally as if he were her long-lost brother. She'd dragged him over to a booth, sat down, then almost breathlessly asked, "Where the hell have you been?"

"Around," he'd told her.

"Mr. Deacon has been trying to reach you for the last two weeks."

"I've been around—didn't think to call Andy—didn't feel like getting back to work. I'll drop in and see him tomorrow," Frost had told her.

"You can't—my God, you *have* been out of touch!"

"What do you mean? What are you talking about?"

"He's out in Los Angeles, some job he wouldn't even tell me about. Took it personally, since he couldn't find you. Said he couldn't trust anyone besides you or himself to do the job."

"Well, then I'll see him when he gets back,"

Frost had said.

"Don't you read the papers? He was shot! Mr. Deacon was gunned down four days ago. He just got out of intensive care. We thought he was going to die. He's still looking for you—as soon as he got conscious he had the nurse call me—'You've gotta find Frost' he had her tell me."

Frost looked again at the cloud cover, then closed his eye, remembering. He had spent another twenty minutes in the bar with Claudia Minish the previous night, then gone to a pay phone and called the hospital where Deacon was. Deacon had been well enough to receive the call after Frost had insisted. But the crusty, ex-FBI agent had sounded weak when Frost spoke with him. Deacon had refused to say why he needed Frost so desperately, insisted he'd pay Frost triple his regular salary. Frost had told him that the money was O.K., but he already had plenty. Then Deacon has used a word Frost had thought wasn't in the man's vocabulary—"please." Finally—he had nothing better to do—Frost had agreed; but Deacon had still insisted he could reveal none of the details by phone. The line was probably tapped.

Frost had worried at that—not about a wiretap, but that perhaps Deacon had finally cracked up. "Why would the line be tapped, Andy?" Frost had asked.

"Why was I gunned down, Hank?"

Frost had said nothing; then after a long silence, Deacon had said, "I gotta get some rest, so I can tell you when I see you. And Hank?"

"Yeah?"

"Come ready for work, huh?"

Frost hadn't had to ask the meaning of the last remark.

He opened his eye, this time staring at his watch—the new Rolex. Maybe if he hadn't given Bess the ring there in the store, and Bess hadn't started to cry, hadn't gone to the bathroom, had been with him instead by the jewelry counter. . . Frost felt in his pocket—the little velvet box was there still. He hadn't wanted to put it away. He took it out, looked at it—part of the finish, the surface of the velvet, was already wearing away. He dropped the box back into his pocket.

Glancing at his new watch again, Frost decided they should be landing at LAX in twenty minutes. He tried to focus his attention on what kind of trouble Deacon had gotten himself into, why Deacon had gotten shot and nearly died. Frost smiled to himself—he didn't really care, but it was something to do, a head game to get his mind going in another direction. That it might be dangerous was of little consequence, he decided. Clinging to life was now more than ever—because of Bess—the last thing on his mind.

He laughed out loud, noticing the man in the seat beside him staring at him. Frost reflected that if he had tried to kill himself after Bess had died, he probably couldn't have done that right. He shook his head, took out a small map and street guide of Los Angeles that he'd put in his coat pocket, and began to study it. Just like the whole trip to bail out Andy Deacon, it was something to do.

Frost felt like a packhorse, sweating in the sun as he walked out of the terminal to the driveway, looking for a taxicab. Slung from his left shoulder was the folded-over suitbag. In his right hand was the black nylon Safariland SWAT bag, in his left hand the locking pistol case—only the KG-9 and its spare magazines in the case now, the Metalified Browning High Power resting under Frost's left armpit in the Alessi shoulder rig.

After talking with Deacon by phone, Frost had stopped by the office with Claudia Minish. The news clippings and the telexed copy of the initial police report indicated Deacon had been walking across a parking lot; three men had come up on him and started shooting. Deacon claimed to have wounded one of the men before getting cut down.

Frost set the black SWAT bag and the pistol case down on the curbstone, looking now for a taxicab, feeling hot in his blue vested suit. He set down the suitbag but it started to tip over. He bent to pick it up. Frost heard the loud popping sound and hit the pavement. There was a scream, another shotgun blast and the sound of glass shattering, then the screech of power steering being pushed too far. Frost was already reaching under his coat as he edged behind the taxicab. He could see the car—a gray sedan, black-wall tires, the license plate dirty and the markings illegible.

Frost left his gun where it was, under his coat, stood up and looked behind him. The first shotgun blast had impacted on a luggage carrier about the height his chest had been before he'd bent over to pick up the suitbag. The second shot column had shattered the window of the taxicab by which he now stood. There were some very quiet, nervous-looking people beside the terminal doors, some of them still on the sidewalk on their knees or flat on their faces, but apparently no one was hurt.

Two uniformed police officers were running down the sidewalk—Frost didn't move.

The policemen ran past him. His hands shaking a little, Frost picked up his bags, then slowly started toward the first cab in the line. The last thing he wanted was to get his name taken as a witness to the shooting, to give his employer as Diablo Protective Services, to get stopped by the police. There was a cold feeling in his stomach now—if Deacon's hospital phone was tapped, that meant somebody or something with connections was involved. Frost hadn't given Deacon his flight number—he hadn't known it at the time. Yet, whoever the shotgunner in the gray sedan was, he'd known Frost on sight, known just where to find Frost and exactly when.

Frost got into the taxicab, rolling down the rear window as a precaution before closing the door.

"Hey—I got the air conditionin' on!"

Frost looked at the driver, leaning forward out of the rear seat as he did. "I'm allergic to air conditioning, but on the other hand I'm a big tipper."

"Where to, mister?"

Frost noticed his own face in the driver's rear-view—he was smiling. Frost sat back all the way in the passenger seat, his right hand under his jacket, the fingertips touching the Pachmayr-gripped butt of the Browning. Frost realized that perhaps he was acting paranoid—rolling the window down to prevent gas or something being leaked into the passenger compartment as it so frequently is in the movies; rolling the window down so he could open the door from the outside if needed.

And holding on to his gun, like some sort of talisman. He heard the cab driver talking, "I asked ya—where to, mister?"

Frost lit a cigarette with the battered Zippo, saying through a cloud of grayish smoke, "Just take me for a ride—I'll tell you later."

It had been the lead cab, would likely be a backup for the shotgunner in the event of a miss on the timing. Frost inhaled hard on the Camel, his eye never leaving the rear-view, watching the eyes of the cab-driver; and as the cab pulled out into traffic watching the green four-door sedan almost causing an accident sliding in three cars behind.

Definitely, Frost thought. Deacon had been in over his head. And Frost wondered if he were too.

Chapter Two

Frost leaned forward in the passenger seat, then quickly, before the cabbie could react, Frost pushed himself up, swinging his right leg over into the front seat. The cabbie started turning toward him as Frost hauled his left leg behind him, plopping down beside the man. Frost's right hand came from under the left side of his suitcoat, the Browning High Power snaking out; Frost's right thumb jacked back the hammer to full stand with an audible double click.

"What the—"

"Relax," Frost rasped. "Those guys in the green car behind us—lose 'em."

The cabbie turned, glaring back at Frost and Frost punched the muzzle of the High Power a few inches closer, up-angling it toward the cabdriver's face. "I said to lose them—now."

"I don't know what you're talkin' about, mister—what's with the—"

"Drive," Frost said, trying to make his voice sound as low and menacing as possible.

"Hey—reach into my jacket pocket—up here," and the cabdriver slowly gestured toward the outside left breast pocket of the battered suede jacket he wore.

Frost reached across the man, keeping the muzzle of the Browning close beside the face as he did.

Frost knew what it was before he opened it, by feel. It was a small, thin wallet. And only one kind of guy carried two wallets, Frost knew—a cop. He opened the wallet. There was no badge—the badge would be somewhere else. The I.D. card was enough—Federal Bureau of Investigation.

"So relax the rod, mister," the cabdriver started.

"So drive," Frost told him, the muzzle of the Browning High Power unflinching.

"Hey—"

"I know, I'm playing with fire. You're a federal officer, the whole nine yards. Like I said, lose the guys in the green car—now!"

Frost didn't gesture with the gun. It was one reason why he liked single-action automatics like the Browning High Power. He could thumb-cock the hammer for dramatic effect. You could do that with a double-action automatic, or a DA revolver too, but that was only a sign of being an amateur. Now, the Browning cocked, the muzzle inches from the FBI-cabdriver's face, there wasn't anything left to do with the gun except pull the trigger and Frost had no intention of doing that. The cabdriver still wasn't accelerating away from the pursuit car.

"You can skip the lecture about when I shoot you, the car goes out of control and we both get killed. I'm close enough to kill the engine and hit the brakes—better still just roll you out onto the street and take the taxi and drive it. Now—you going to show me how good Uncle Sam trains FBI guys to drive or do I dump you? No more talk. Your move."

Frost looked at the man; the man looked at him. "Damn you," the cabdriver snapped, then glanced over his shoulder; then into the mirrors and hit the gas pedal, the Plymouth's engine starting to drone louder, the sounds of the transmission kicking into high, audible over it. Frost shot a glance behind him—the cab was cutting through the airport exit-ramp traffic, the green car suddenly starting to accelerate behind them. "Look—I don't know anything about that green car, Frost—not a damned thing."

"Terrific—then we both want to lose it—I'll just lean back and relax," but Frost never moved the muzzle of the pistol.

"Listen, Frost—I'll give you some advice—I read your record. You're O.K."

"It's sweet of you to say so." Frost smiled.

"Listen, damn it—I'm trying to help ya out. You'll never get to Deacon, and you know it."

"Why?"

"What do you mean, why? You know—" But then the cabbie stopped, cutting the wheel into a sharp left on a yellow light across an intersection, a surfer-painted van just missing sideswiping them. As the cabdriver corrected, accelerated down a wide palm-studded boulevard, Frost looked behind them again. The green car was still coming, but it looked, from the block or so distance, that the green car hadn't been quite so lucky at the intersection—the left front fender was peeled back.

"Why shouldn't I see Deason?" Frost rasped, looking back at the FBI man behind the wheel, beside him.

"You don't know what's goin' on then—you really don't!"

"What the hell are you talkin' about?" Frost snapped, looking behind over the front seat back, studying the green car—it was starting to gain on them. "Those guys in the green sedan are startin' to make time. Better boogie, pal," and Frost fumbled a Camel from his coat pocket with his left hand, then lit it quickly in the blue-yellow flame of his battered Zippo.

"Deacon," the FBI man snapped. "He's into something he shouldn't have gotten into. He's working with the Commies. I don't know if he knows it or not. I never met him, but heard he was a good fed. But whether he knows it or not, he's working with the Reds, and he wants you to do it, too. If you don't know anything about it, Frost—then hop the next plane out of here and disappear someplace fast—maybe that girl friend your file says you got back in London."

Frost inhaled hard, almost choking on the cigarette smoke. His voice low, his gun hand trembling, Frost snapped, "You'd better update the file, pal—a terrorist bombing in a department store there killed her. And you mention her again and you're gonna wish a terrorist bombing had killed you."

The cabdriver snapped his head right, looking at Frost; then, the man's voice low, said, "Sorry, fella—I didn't—"

"What about Deacon?" Frost rasped, glancing back behind them. The green sedan wasn't any closer, but it wasn't any greater distance back either.

"I can't tell you that—if you don't know already. My job was to keep you from getting to the hospital."

"What about those shooters with the shotguns?"

"Not mine—we don't play that game."

"What about the CIA?"

"I don't know anything about the CIA—they don't get involved in domestic intelligence activities. You know that—"

"Bullshit they don't. Was it them?"

"I don't know," the FBI man snapped, glancing at Frost, then back out the windshield.

Frost looked behind the cab. The green sedan was still there.

"You better lose those suckers—now," Frost rasped.

The FBI man looked at Frost, then muttered, "Maybe I read you wrong, maybe you are in on this deal Deacon's got. I guess when you guys go bad, you go all the way. You can damned well—"

Frost cut him off. "Look—if Andy Deacon is into something, you can damned well bet he's on the same side you are. He may not be Mr. Excitement, he may not be the perfect drinking buddy, but there's one thing he is—honest. And don't you go calling me something you're not willing to spit out. If those aren't FBI guys behind us, then you stand just as good a chance of gettin' croaked out of this as I do—so drive."

The FBI man looked at him a moment, then cut the wheel hard left, Frost slid across the seat, then started to react, thinking in that instant that the man driving the cab was making a play. But the cabdriver cut the wheel back right, passing an eighteen-wheeler and sliding through a yellow light across an intersection. The humming of the car's engine made it apparent—the FBI man, this time for real, was trying to lose the green pursuit car.

The taxi turned hard right off the boulevard. Frost glanced ahead of them as the taxi entered an industrial park. Frost started to move the High Power toward the FBI man at the wheel. "Relax, Frost—I know this town better than a real cabbie. There's an alley leading between two factories just up ahead. A couple of years ago, the one factory bought out the other and they closed up the end of the alley. But to keep the trash-removal people happy, they ran off a ramp from the left side of the alley as you drive in. If you miss it, you can follow the alley for two blocks and it dead ends on you. If you miss that turnoff, you're stuck."

"What if the guys in the green car know the city as well as you do?"

"Then we don't lose 'em, I guess—but you can't fault a guy for tryin'."

Frost could already see the alley looming up ahead of them between two massive stucco-fronted factory buildings. A sign on the one on the right read, FIMBERTON MEAT PROCESSORS. Frost looked from the sign to the FBI man driving the cab. "I hope that sign isn't prophetic!"

The FBI man cut a sharp right and they were into the alley. Already the ramp on the left side loomed ahead of them. "Damn it," the FBI man shouted. Frost didn't ask why—the upper portion of the ramp was blocked by what looked like double wooden doors.

"Take the ramp anyway," Frost commanded.

"You're nuts," the FBI man shouted back.

"Do it," Frost told him, brandishing the Browning.

"Hold on," the driver shouted then, cutting the wheel half-left and accelerating up the ramp.

Frost tucked down between the dashboard and the front seat, by the firewall; the sound of the taxicab impacting against the wooden doors was loud, almost deafening, wood and metal tearing against one another—but no sound of glass shattering other than the tinkling of the headlights that shattered just at impact.

The cab lurched to a halt. Frost looked up. The FBI man behind the wheel of the taxicab gripped the steering wheel in white-knuckled fists, his body shaking. "We could have been—"

"But we weren't," Frost interrupted. "Now," and Frost glanced behind them. There was still no sign of the green pursuit car. "Back this thing up, down the ramp, then head up the alley—quick."

The FBI man shot a glance toward Frost, the ashen look in the man's face gone for an instant. "Gotcha—ha!"

The cab was moving, a high-speed reverse over the debris of the broken wooden doors and down the ramp, the FBI man half-propped against the front seat back, his right arm extended, his left hand shifting the wheel of the cab back and forth, right and left. They hit the bottom of the ramp, the taxi's brakes screeching, the transmission thumping as the FBI man shifted too fast out of reverse and into drive, then hit the gas pedal. The car stalled for a second, then lurched forward with a screech as the wheels spun out and straightened. As they rounded the first curve in the alley, Frost could see the nose of the green car, turning in behind them.

"Stop this thing," Frost commanded. As the driver hit the brakes, Frost felt himself getting thrown slightly forward.

"What?"

"Shut up—I'm counting," Frost snapped. ". . . One thousand nine, one thousand ten, one thousand eleven, one thousand twelve, one thousand thirteen, one thousand fourteen, one thousand fifteen—" Then Frost glanced back behind them, snapping to the driver. "O.K.—back her up fast and out of the alley."

"What the—you think they bought it?"

"No time like the present to find out," Frost answered, not looking at the man.

The FBI man edged around in the driver's seat,

his right arm across the seat back again, the cab already in reverse. The engine whined as the taxi accelerated back down the alley. The Browning High Power was clinched tight in Frost's right fist—in case the green sedan hadn't taken the bait of the broken-down wooden doors and taken the ramp out of the alley.

The ramp was in sight now, more of the wood from the doors hanging off the high sides of the ramp and into the alley below—there was no green car in sight though—behind them or, as Frost craned his neck up and peered through the windshield, on the ramp.

The taxicab was still accelerating, reversing out of the narrow driveway, the FBI man behind the wheel saying, "Looks like they bought the whole nine yards—now if you're smart, Frost, you'll take this taxicab right back to the airport."

"Yeah—so you can get me arrested." Frost smiled, the muzzle of the Browning still trained on the man.

"Hey—no, I—"

Frost leaned across the front seat, his face inches from the FBI man's face as the taxi wheeled back out of the alley, cut a reverse right and skidded to a stop. "Take me to the hospital, pal."

"You'll never get in."

Frost, his voice low and emotionless, almost whispered, "You'd better hope I do, and that I get out. You and I are walking into that hospital together, going to Deacon's room and going inside. You make one wrong move and you're dead. You do anything to alert the people guarding Deacon or get up a SWAT team or anything like that and there's a shoot-out—well, you're dead too.''

"You wouldn't smoke a fed, not if you got an ounce of—''

"Remember that file of mine that needed updating? Well, with my 'London girl friend' gone, you might say maybe I've got a death wish or somethin'. You just try crossing me and see if you live long.''

The FBI man stared back at Frost, and in the man's eyes Frost saw something he hadn't seen there before—fear. Frost wondered what the man saw in his eye. Was the death wish really there? Frost remembered waking up, learning that Bess had been killed, wishing he had never awakened. Maybe that was the reason he'd taken Deacon's message, left London in the first place. At the moment, there was no lead to who had triggered the terrorist bomb; there was nothing he could do. It wasn't a need for action, Frost thought, watching the FBI man getting the cab going back out onto the wide, palm-studded boulevard. Maybe, Frost thought, maybe he was hoping for something, looking for something, wishing for something—to put him out of his own misery. Bess . . .

Frost had slipped the Metalifed Browning High Power back into the Alessi rig under his suit jacket, but he held the Gerber MkI boot knife cupped in his left hand, the blade extending up his sleeve. He'd told the FBI man driving the cab that one wrong move would get Frost to hammer the knife into the man's kidney. Frost knew that was the last thing he would do, but didn't think the FBI man knew it.

They'd parked the cab in the lot and gone through the front entrance, taking the stairs to the third floor where Frost had gotten the man to admit Deacon's room was. Frost had opted for the stairs out of simple reason—he could be trapped less easily in a stairwell than in an elevator. But there was no trap—at least not yet—as Frost stepped through the stairwell door onto the third floor by the nurses' station. He could see a young uniformed L.A. police officer sitting in front of the room nearest the nursing station. Frost's eye gravitated to the duty belt—some type of stainless Smith & Wesson revolver in one of the Bianchi Break Front holsters.

Frost edged against the FBI man, the FBI man's three-inch-barreled Smith Model 13 long since stuck into Frost's waistband. "Let's go," the one-eyed man rasped.

"You're nuts—that cop's gonna nail your—"

"Better hope he doesn't." Frost smiled, already starting to walk; the FBI man—haltingly—walked with him.

They walked past the nurses' station, Frost smiling at the white-capped woman in a white pantsuit uniform. "Remember the drill," Frost rasped to the FBI man.

"And what if I don't, Frost?"

Frost kept smiling. "I've got your gun, my gun, and this knife—maybe I won't get too far, but neither will you, that cop, anybody who tries to stop me."

"Bite my—"

"You're not my type." Frost laughed.

They stopped three feet away from the young

black cop watching the door. Frost read the name tag—he couldn't believe his eye, blinked, and read it again; the tag read, FRIENDLY.

"Officer Friendly?"

"Yes, sir," the young man answered, already on his feet.

"My name is Cullom—I'm with Special Agent Boyd here," Frost told the police officer.

"That's, ahh, that's right, Officer Friendly," the FBI man said, his voice sounding tight and strained. "Here's my I.D.—want to question Mr. Deacon if he's awake?"

"I think he is, sir," the young black cop answered, taking the I.D. case a moment, scrutinizing it, then stepping aside from the door as he handed back the case.

Reaching out with his right hand, the left one concealing the knife still at his side, Frost almost shoved the FBI man ahead of him, as they started to the door. He got the doorknob in his fist, turned it, and letting the FBI man, Boyd, ahead of him, started through the door. Frost turned to Officer Friendly, "Ahh—please don't let anyone disturb us."

"Yes, sir." The officer smiled, stepping back behind Frost as Frost closed the door.

Frost could see Deacon sitting propped up on the bed, eyes closed, an i.v. tube leading out of his left arm; the arm was heavily bandaged.

Frost scanned the room, seeing no immediate evidence of closed-circuit television cameras.

"Now what?" The FBI man turned toward Frost who already had the little three-inch Smith .357 out in his right hand.

"Well?"

"Is he asleep?"

"How the hell should I know?" And Boyd, the FBI man, turned half-around to look at Deacon. As he did, Frost brought the round butt of the little revolver down right behind the FBI man's left ear.

"Sorry, pal," Frost muttered, dropping the revolver into his suitcoat pocket and catching the FBI man under the armpits to keep him from hitting his head on the hard floor.

Frost dragged the man half-across the room, leaving black heel marks on the polished floor. He inched Boyd into a pink vinyl chair, the unconscious agent's head lolling forward onto the chest. Frost continued talking, as though Boyd were still conscious. "Looks like Deacon's asleep, Boyd—all this way for nothing. I want to wait a few minutes though and see if he wakes up." As Frost talked—to himself—he searched the room, this time giving a more detailed look to make certain no cameras were present. To search without mechanical aid for optical fibers would have been too time consuming and the chances of total success would have been poor, Frost realized. He looked for microphones, too, still keeping up the imaginary conversation with the unconscious Special Agent Boyd. Deacon was starting to stir, his eyes opening, their lids fluttering.

Then Deacon turned his head, the eyes—a little bloodshot—wide open, staring at Frost. Frost touched a finger to his lips, gesturing him to silence, as he continued his conversation. "Let's give it a couple more minutes, Boyd—see if Deacon wakes up." Frost rustled the pages of a magazine on the night stand beside Deacon's bed. "Here, Boyd, read a magazine—good for your mind." Then Frost made a low grunt as if Boyd were saying something.

And then Frost found the microphone—in the nurse call switch beside Deacon's pillow, clipped to the end of the casing. Frost didn't touch the device; instead, silently, he eased Deacon's head up and slid the pillow from underneath it, then slowly, carefully cushioned the pillow over the microphone.

Frost looked at Deacon, smiled, and whispered, "I'd say it's good to see you, Andy, but that'd be a lie."

"Frost—you came. Thank God."

"Well, don't thank the FBI," Frost murmured, gesturing toward Boyd. Frost handed Deacon Boyd's gun. "Here—when I leave, keep this guy covered if he starts to wake up too soon. Now what have you got yourself into?"

"I'll pay you twenty-five thousand bucks, Hank—twice what I should pay."

"Fine—the money is nice, but I won't die without it. Now—what's up? Why the FBI, the CIA maybe, maybe some other people? Who shot you—who pot-shotted at me near the airport?"

"Then they're onto you!" Deacon exclaimed, wide-eyed. Frost studied the pupils briefly—dilated. Probably the medication, he thought.

His tone softening, Frost asked, "How are you doin'—I mean, you gonna be all right?"

"Yeah—in a few weeks I guess. I'm not gonna run any races for a while though," and Deacon gestured feebly with his bandaged right hand toward his leg.

"What happened?"

"Three guys—I knew what they were out to do, a bag job, put the snatch on me to tell 'em where she was. So I forced the fight. I nailed one of the guys, but he got away—but if *I* was in bad shape, he was worse. Submachine gun did this to me," and he made an expansive gesture with his bandaged right hand again, the hand dropping to his side on the bed.

"Why, Andy—what the hell has the FBI got out for you?"

"You ever hear of Calvin Plummer?"

Frost thought a moment. "Some guy with the CIA—right?"

"He heads a special, almost autonomous branch of the intelligence fraternity, loosely tied to Central Intelligence." Frost felt like yawning at Deacon—he was sounding like an official report. "He runs deep-cover, covert-operations agents. It was decided several years ago that one man should be responsible for managing the deep-cover people, be responsible for them, have total authority for their operations. Well, Plummer is the guy. We haven't been doing too well in that field of covert operations, really. But Plummer's had this one girl planted in KGB now for five years, girl by the name of Jessica Pace, substituting for a KGB agent named Irena Pavarova. They're perfect duplicates for one another, identical to the smallest detail."

"So?" Frost groaned.

"So—she's coming in from the cold."

"Aww, cut the spy-story stuff, huh." Frost moaned.

"All right—she's coming back from Russia—all right?"

Frost smiled. Deacon seemed to be getting his wind back.

"Anyway, she blew her own cover identity intentionally—she had to."

"I don't follow you," Frost complained.

"She found a list, Frost—that's why I'm in on this and they shot me, why they want her dead, why I need your help."

"Who are they?" Frost asked slowly, then without waiting for an answer, pointed at Boyd, the FBI man. "They?"

Deacon—overly solemn Frost thought—nodded. "Some of them. The list is a master list stolen from Calvin Plummer's opposite number in the Soviet Union." Frost groaned again at the spy-lingo double-talk—opposite number. "It's a list of all the double agents holding positions of trust and authority in the FBI and Central Intelligence Agency. And it's a big list, Hank—Plummer trusted me enough to tell me that."

"Why didn't he give you a bulletproof vest instead of a merit badge?" Frost asked, feeling the corners of his mouth down-turning in a sour expression under his mustache.

"This is one of the greatest responsibilities any American could ever be trusted with, Hank," Deacon said sincerely.

"So why are you trusting me with it?" Frost cracked.

Deacon didn't smile. "I need to get the job done, and I heard about Bess dying. I guess I figured I

37

could trust your loyalty and your, ahh—"

Deacon was stammering; Frost felt his face getting hot, saying, "You figured if I had to die doing this it wouldn't bother me much—right?"

"No, I ahh—"

"Bullshit!"

"O.K.—they got me, they can get you. I needed somebody I could trust—the money's good, you're the mercenary, I thought that's what you looked for," Deacon snapped.

Frost looked at his on-again, off-again boss from Diablo. "Yeah, the money's good, all right," Frost whispered, still mindful of the mike covered with the pillow. "But it doesn't really matter, does it," and Frost looked at the FBI man, Boyd, still unconscious on the chair. "After cold-cocking the fed, forcing him to get me in here—hell. . . The only way I can get out of goin' to the slam for thirty years is to get that broad—what's her name?"

"Jessica Pace," Deacon said emotionlessly.

". . . Jessica Pace where she's gotta go—isn't it?" Frost didn't wait for an answer. "And where is it she's gotta go, anyway?"

"To Washington—"

"D.C.?" Frost interrupted incredulously.

"Yeah—and all the airports, train stations—everything will be watched."

"We walk, right?"

"Drive it out—the only way, I think."

"Where's she to go in Washington—Plummer?"

"You'll notify him—but she goes straight to the President, reports only to him. Like I said, Hank—that list's got some big names on it."

"What about these guys?" And Frost gestured toward the FBI man in the chair.

"My guess—and Plummer warned me it could happen—was the big guys in FBI and CIA put out some kind of cover story of their own on Jessica Pace. The ones who know who she is and what she's carrying in her head will be back of it, out to kill her and with whatever story they've got trumped up, probably have all the legitimate guys in both agencies gunning for her too. That's why Plummer called me—he knew me, trusted me, and admitted frankly that he didn't know who he could trust in the government—the list of traitors was so pervasive."

"So all the way from here to Washington," Frost began, his own voice sounding tired to him, "I'll have the FBI and the CIA on my tail."

"And the KGB—they put a lot of effort into working those moles they got in the company and the bureau."

"Moles," Frost thought, saying it half-aloud. "Cut the spy crap, huh? So the KGB too," Frost spit out in desperation.

"Yeah—the KGB, the FBI, and the CIA—all of 'em, and probably every local cop between here and there too."

Frost started to say something, then looked at Deacon—he figured at least three more weeks in the hospital for the man, barring complications. Frost decided if there was one malady he was expert at, it was gunshot wounds. Then there was the FBI man—Boyd. Unintentionally, Frost had committed himself to the point where he couldn't just walk away from it anymore.

Throwing his hands up, walking across the room toward the window, he rasped, "All right!" Then, turning back to Deacon, "Where is she—give me all the poop on how to contact Plummer, too."

Frost started back toward the bed, then stopped, looking Deacon square in the face. "How come with you here they haven't, ahh," and Frost gestured in the air.

"Shot me up, squirted the truth drugs—couldn't without risking the local cops getting in on what Plummer told me. Oddly enough, I'm halfway safe here."

I'm all smiles, Frost thought.

"Gimme a matchbook, Hank," Deacon began.

Frost reached into his pockets with both hands, finding a half-dead matchbook from the airport restaurant where he'd boarded the jet. He handed it to Deacon.

"You got a pen?"

"Ohh, yeah—just a minute, old friend and pal," Frost cracked. He fished into his pockets, found a Cross pen and looked at it—Bess had given it to him.

"Damn it," Frost cursed, throwing the pen onto Deacon's sheet-covered lap.

Frost pounded his right fist into his left hand—he wanted a cigarette, but the oxygen tank in the corner made him think better of it. He lit the cigarette anyway—if he blew up the hospital room, Frost decided, he couldn't be any worse off.

Chapter Three

"Yeah, Boyd, I'll be right back—you and Deacon talk there," Frost shouted, the door into the hospital corridor half-open as he said it. Boyd was still unconscious, but Frost decided that wouldn't prohibit Deacon from having an animated conversation with the man. Many was the time, Frost reflected, that Deacon had been talking to him about a Diablo Protective Services job and for all intents and purposes Deacon had been talking to an unconscious man. Deacon had a certain quality that endowed everything with a kind of unanimity, the power to make a report about Martians landing in an active volcano and kidnapping naked women sound like a supply report.

Frost closed the door, the matchbook with the location of the woman—Jessica Pace—and the contact route for reaching Plummer written inside it stuck inside the cellophane outside wrapping of the half-smoked pack of Camels in his coat pocket.

Frost turned, starting past the policeman.

"Just a minute, sir."

Frost turned around, smiled as pleasantly as he could. "Yes, Officer Friendly?" He couldn't help it—he laughed.

"What the hell is so funny?"

"Nothing," Frost enthused. "Not a thing! Honest!"

"Before you go, sir," the young man began, his voice deep-sounding. "I'd just like to take a look inside that room."

"Sure," Frost answered, his palms sweating.

As the young policeman started to turn, Frost's right hand snaked under his coat, ripping the Metalifed High Power 9-mm from the leather, the gun already cocked and locked, his right thumb swiping down the manual safety.

"Freeze, Officer Friendly," Frost snapped.

The policeman started to move, then stopped, his hands inches from the butt of the stainless-steel revolver in his hip holster.

"What's that—a Model 67?"

"Yeah—Combat Masterpiece Stainless. What's it to you?"

"Well, you just take that Combat Masterpiece Stainless .38 out of that holster nice and

42

slow—break it through the lips there nice and easy and don't let me see your hand go on that trigger guard or anywhere near it. Capiche, Officer Friendly?''

''The holster—it—''

''I know,'' Frost smiled. ''You gotta break the gun out the front, down and forward, but do it slow. I've got no reason to smoke you, but I will—promise.''

Frost never took his eye off the young black policeman's eyes as the man started the gun from the leather. ''Now—hand it over.''

The policeman—Officer Friendly—looked at him angrily. ''And what if I don't?''

Frost said nothing, just inched the muzzle of the Browning closer to the policeman.

Officer Friendly eased the gun butt down and passed the gun ahead of him, Frost taking it around the black Pachmayr grips in his left hand, then shoving it in his belt.

''The gun'll be down the stairwell some-place—you'll find it. But don't follow me—right?''

''You know I gotta,'' the man said, his voice deep-sounding, tight.

''Yeah,'' Frost rasped. ''I know—but it didn't hurt to try, huh?''

''Yeah—I know.''

Frost edged back, away from the black cop—Officer Friendly. The young man's body was coiled like a spring, ready to pounce at the slightest chance, the kind of kinetic energy, Frost thought, that you saw in actors in 1930s movies. The simple thing, the one-eyed man realized, would have been to get the young police officer to turn around, then pull the light switch on him as he had done with Boyd, the FBI man. But something inside Frost—which he promptly labeled as stupid—kept him from doing that to this intelligent-seeming young man with the abysmally absurd name—Officer Friendly.

Frost saw the nurse at her station, out of the corner of his eye, start for a telephone. "Give me a break, huh—make it sporting and wait to call for help until I hit the stairwell, huh?"

Frost winked at her. She smiled, almost looking embarrassed that she had.

Frost stopped, his back beside the stairwell door—Three floors down, he thought. The elevator would be quicker, but also easier to trap him in. He wondered just how fast he could make it down six half-flights of stairs, taking into account that as soon as he was through the door, the nurse would be on her telephone and the young police officer would be right behind him.

"Bye!" Frost smiled, shoving through the panic-locked door and into the stairwell.

He stood right beside the door, expecting the police officer to charge through, to figure Frost was now running down the stairs for his life.

Frost waited, almost holding his breath.

Frost set the young officer's gun down on the landing in the corner, emptying it first and pocketing the six rounds of ammo.

The door creaked open, then burst wide, and the young black officer was streaking through it and on-to the landing, starting for the first step before Frost rasped, "Officer Friendly?"

The young man spun half-around, starting to reach out for Frost. Frost's right foot came up, the toe smashing forward into the policeman's stomach—something made Frost feel like not seriously hurting the guy. Friendly doubled forward, Frost's right fist hooking up. The one-eyed man rasped, "Hope you got a strong jaw, pal," and Frost's knuckles impacted against the tip of the policeman's chin. The man started to fall back, into the stairwell; Frost grabbed at the officer's shirt front and tie, hauling him back, feeling the young policeman's legs buckling. Frost shook his head—the man was still conscious, his hands swinging, attempting to fight.

Frost laced him once across the jaw with his left and wheeled him around, letting him sink to the floor in the corner of the landing beside his gun.

"You're a good man, Officer Friendly," Frost snapped, starting down the stairs now as fast as he could. Frost had always secretly admired the guys he'd seen throughout his lifetime who could take steps two or three at a time on the way down—Frost just wasn't that coordinated, he realized.

He was on the second-floor landing by the time he heard the sirens starting outside the hospital. He smiled, hoping nobody was sleeping. "The hell with it," he rasped, flipping the railing from the next stair flight to the flight below that, almost twisting his right ankle. "Won't try that again," he snapped, hitting the next landing, swinging around it, and starting to the first-floor stairwell door. On impulse, he pulled it open fast—two police officers were starting through it to cut him off. Frost grabbed for the first man, again not wanting to kill, blocking a swinging right from a fist holding a dark wood night stick. The stick cracked hollowly against the wall beside Frost's head. Frost lashed out with his right fist and clipped the policeman across the jaw. The second cop was starting for him and as the first man went down, Frost grabbed the night stick from the limp right fist of the first man. As the second cop's stick crashed down, Frost half-rolled to his right, blocking the night stick blow with the stick from the first policeman.

Frost edged back as the cop swung the stick in his right hand like a scimitar. The night stick Frost held was in both his hands and when the police officer recovered and started crashing the night stick down again, Frost blocked it, then took a half-step in, toward the man's body. Frost's left knee smashed upward; the police officer half-turned to avoid the blow. But Frost's knee hadn't been aiming for the abdomen or groin. Frost's left leg stopped halfway to the target, his foot kicking out, into the policeman's right knee. There was a rush of air and a groan from the copy as he started to buckle back. Frost snapped the butt of the night stick he held forward, into the tip of the policeman's jaw, letting the man fall, and turned to the doorway.

There were at least six police officers—that was all he had time to count—storming toward him. Frost shouted at the top of his lungs and hurled the borrowed night stick. All six policemen ducked, one of them going for his gun.

Frost started to run toward the main hospital

46

doors, but two policemen blocked his way. He knew better than to expect them to use their guns in the crowded hospital main floor. He rushed them; the two men—one of them bigger than Frost by a good thirty pounds—stood shoulder to shoulder between him and the door. Frost extended his hands and shouted, a karate-type yell. Both men raised their guards, expecting, he guessed, a martial-arts attack. Frost drew his pistol; both men started for theirs, but their raised hands were too far away from their belts to make their draws.

"Out of my way or I croak ya'—so help me," Frost snapped. The smaller of the two cops stood his ground a moment longer than the larger man—short guys were like that sometimes Frost thought—and he edged between the men and started through the glass doors into the circular driveway. Then he started to run hard—outside the hospital there'd be nothing to stop the police from shooting.

"Get him!" Frost heard somebody yell from behind him as he hit the sidewalk on the far side of the driveway—he mentally bet it was the short guy. There was a gunshot behind him; the pavement beside his feet was chewed up from the impact of a slug. Frost jumped like a runner in a track meet—but instead of a hurdle it was a hedgerow. He cleared it, hearing another shot from behind him, then dived to the ground into a roll, the Browning High Power still in his right fist. He snapped off two fast shots, aiming high, hearing the sound of glass shattering, then shouts from some of the policemen pursuing him. "He's got a gun!"

Frost wondered what they thought it was he'd

been shooting. He fired two more shots, then scrambled to his feet, starting in a dead run across the grass fronting the hospital main building and flanked on his left by the driveway leading past the emergency room and out into the street.

"Get that son of a—" Frost snapped two shots over his left shoulder half-wheeling, intentionally shooting high. He glanced from side to side, trying to determine where to run. Far along the grassy area, beyond the furthest extension of the hospital building itself, he could see a long greenway, almost like a golf course. He laughed as he started to run—it had to be the perfect hospital, the doctors could play golf while they were on duty. He started running for it, his hands low at his sides, his shoulders thrown back, his lungs already starting to ache, his shins cramping. . . . He thought of the time he'd spent in London going around the bars, the pubs, hanging around the offices of New Scotland Yard, searching for a lead on the terrorist bombing. . . . Bess, he thought, his mouth wide open, panting for breath as he ran, feeling the tightness in his throat that wasn't from the running . . .

He could hear more shouting behind him. Wheeling, he snapped off two shots at a phalanx of pursuing policemen; the officers almost dutifully ducked to avoid his gunfire. He ran again, crossing past the far corner of the hospital building and into the greenway, temporarily out of their line of fire until the police crossed into the greenway as well.

Frost stopped, bending double, his belly aching, his breath coming in short gasps. Sweat streamed down his brow, under his eye patch; his hair was plastered to his forehead. He looked ahead of him, felt a breeze cooling him, then started running again, across the greenway and into what looked almost like a park beyond it, tree-studded; a small wooden bridge loomed up ahead of him.

The police officers were rounding the corner of the building; Frost dived for cover in a depression in the grassy ground as they fired. Still trying not to connect, not to kill a policeman, Frost fired—two rounds, then two more—firing low into the ground in front of the dozen police officers, then into the air as they dived for cover.

Frost looked around the greenway—there was no cover. He'd still have to run, he knew. Pushing himself up on his hands and knees, then to his feet, he took off in a low, dead run, toward the small wooden bridge.

"There he goes," Frost heard someone shout. Instinctively, he dived toward the base of the bridge, gunfire from the police service revolvers hammering around him, into the ground and the rough wooden bridge supports. Frost rolled down a small embankment, sliding in the dirt; his feet stopped at the base of the small grade. He looked down. "Damn it," he rasped. His sixty-five-dollar shoes were awash with water. He mentally shrugged—if you were going to have a bridge, it only made sense to have it be a bridge over something. He pumped two rounds toward the police officers, the dozen or so men firing back almost in unison. The ground in front of Frost's face was torn up, pieces of dirt and sod spraying against his face and his hands. Frost fired again. The Browning's magazine wasn't empty yet, but he took the moment to swap for a full magazine anyway, dropping the partially spent Metalifed magazine into his side jacket pocket. Fourteen rounds in the pistol, he pushed away from the embankment, following the shallow water away from the shelter of the bridge; his feet sloshed in the stream.

It was a small stream, and at the far end there was another low embankment. Above it he could see a low, wrought-iron fence, more ornamental, he thought, than for security. He started running again, along the water's edge and toward the embankment, clambering up the side, his feet slipping because his shoes were wet. As he slid down, his face grated against the gravel embankment; Frost pushed himself up with his hands. His palms felt as though he were pushing against broken glass. He squinted his eye against the sun and looked below the fence through an opening in the hedgerow. "Naw," he rasped. Frost pushed himself up over the lip of the embankment, then half-stumbled toward the fence. He could hear the sounds of voices behind him, the sounds of someone thrashing through the shallow stream, as he pushed through the hedgerow. His trouser leg caught on a thorn, ripping. Having shoved the Browning into his belt, he grabbed the fence with both fists, and started to haul himself up. The side of his jacket caught and tore on one of the ornamental spikes; then Frost dropped over onto the other side.

It was a sanitarium; white-uniformed nurses and orderlies stood behind or beside wheelchairs—the people, arranged almost like pieces on a chessboard, all started toward him. Hearing the sounds of voices getting louder, he glanced behind him, then started to run.

"Get out of the way—look out!" Frost shouted.

No one moved. He looked behind him, to where the nurses and patients and orderlies were staring. Almost as if they'd rehearsed it, ten of the twelve policemen who'd run after him were flipping over the fence.

Frost wing-shot the High Power over their heads. One of the officers tripped as he cleared the fence; the others ducked into the bushes or flattened themselves on the ground. Someone shouted, "Don't shoot—look out."

A smile crossed Frost's lips. He thought if he could have seen his own smile in a mirror he would have called it wicked.

He started running again, toward the center of the knot of old people and hospital workers.

"Halt! Halt!" There was a shot and Frost spun around, seeing a policeman in the center of his pursuers with a service revolver still pointed muzzle-skyward. Frost started to turn, to run. There were hands grabbing at his shoulders and he wheeled, staring into watery gray eyes in a face that was a field of wrinkles.

"Hold it, boy!"

The man had to be eighty, but the eyes, despite their wateriness, were dead serious.

Frost looked at the man. Then, controlling his voice, making it dead serious, he whispered in a confidential tone, "I'm really an apprentice G-man and this is a training film—relax."

There was a puzzled look in the eyes and Frost shrugged off the restraining hands as gently as he could, then started running again.

He saw what he wanted—a fence, on the far side of the sanitarium grounds.

Frost ran dead-out—the Browning High Power cocked and locked in his right fist—hearing the shouts of the policemen behind him, nurses screaming, some of the old people shouting; one of them laughing, another screaming, "Right on!"

Frost hit the fence, rammed the pistol into his trouser band, and jumped, getting hold of the top of the fence. He felt something holding his left ankle. He looked down—at a white-coated orderly with curly blond hair and a look of determination in his face. Frost kicked him with his right foot square in the look of determination, then flipped the top of the fence.

Frost hit the ground, but it wasn't level and he started to roll, snatching at his gun as he splayed out on the ground at the base of a low embankment. He pushed himself up; then ran toward the parking lot a hundred yards to his left. All he could see were police cars. One had the Mars lights on, the doors open. He spotted four policemen disappearing around the far corner of the lot—evidently having just run from the car.

Frost heard somebody shouting. "Shit, Larry! You left the motor runnin'!"

Frost hit the police car, almost throwing himself behind the wheel. Cranking the stick into reverse, he cut a wide arc to his right, then threw the transmission into drive. He started out of the lot; the rubber creeched as he stomped hard on the accelerator. The cops who'd been following him were running toward him; one of them threw himself on the hood of the car. Frost stomped hard on the brakes, then threw the car into reverse, cutting another wide arc. The cop fell off the hood of the patrol car; the front passenger door caught on the fender of another police car and tore away.

Frost got the transmission into drive again, then hammered the gas pedal down under his soggy right shoe. He heard and felt the leather squish, then lost the sound in the roar of the engine. The driver's side door slammed closed as he wheeled hard right out of the parking lot into the street.

There were police cars blocking the far end of the street, but Frost didn't worry about them—he wasn't going that way, he knew. He cut the wheel into another hard right, into the rear of the hospital driveway, toward the far parking lot where he'd left the taxicab.

He could see it ahead of him. Cutting the wheel hard left, he peeled off the police car's left front fender on a concrete abutment. Then, cutting the wheel right, he stomped hard on the brakes, threw the gearshift lever into park, and half-fell out of the squad car.

"The keys! What the—" But Frost found the taxicab keys in his trouser pockets, fumbled the door lock and crammed inside behind the wheel.

He pumped the pedal, turned the key; the taxi didn't start. He tried it again. The car started, then stalled out. "Flooded," he muttered, looking over the hood of the taxi, watching as the squad cars closed into the parking lot, seeing the policemen who were on foot converging on him. "Patience," he muttered; then counted to ten, forced a smile, and slowly turned the key. The engine rumbled to life and Frost touched the fingers of his left hand to his lips and planted a kiss on the dashboard.

He revved the engine, then before it slowed, was already hauling the cab into reverse.

There was a drag. He released the emergency brake; the cab lurched backward—too fast. He hammered into the front end of the nearest squad car, before he worked the shift into drive, stomped on the gas, and started across the parking lot.

There were two police cars, wheeling to a half a hundred yards in front of him. Frost cut a sharp right, bouncing off another police car just parked there, then started diagonally across the parking lot. There was a grassy hill on the far side and he didn't know what was beyond it. He got his right foot all the way to the floor and started toward it, the taxi-cab bounced up over the low curb, then ground up the grassy hill. Frost couldn't see anything past the top, and then he was there. The hill dropped off and Frost felt a sickening feeling in his stomach as the taxi sailed through midair, every bone in his body shuddering as the taxi impacted.

"My God—I'm alive," he rasped, then pounded his foot to the floor. He was back on the broad palm-lined boulevard and he didn't understand how. There was honking, shouting, and he realized he was driving against the flow of traffic. He tapped the brake pedal, cut the wheel hard left, and skidded from a sloppy bootlegger turn up and over the grassy area separating the two-way traffic. Bouncing into the opposite lanes, he joined the flow of cars.

Miraculously, there wasn't a police car behind him, and he had no desire to push his luck. Frost hauled the cab into the far right lane and made the first right, then turned down an alley. He could hear sirens in the distance. He didn't wait for them. Reaching into the rear seat he snatched up his luggage and ran toward the far end of the alley. There Frost sank into a heap behind a fence, caught his breath, then boosted himself up and looked over—a Doberman lunged up toward him, missing his left hand by less than an inch as he let go of the fence top and dropped back into the alley.

Frost grabbed up his baggage and started to run again. He could still hear the Doberman barking and yelping so he turned his head to shout, "Sorry!"

Chapter Four

Having found the nearest good-sized men's clothing store and purchased a pair of slacks as an excuse to use the dressing room, Frost left his luggage temporarily behind the cashier's desk and changed out of his ripped and grass-stained blue three-piece suit. The slacks weren't bad, really, but the price had been a little inflated he'd thought—and besides, he hadn't needed them, just the place to change. He'd told the clerk who'd waited on him that he'd been the victim of muggers whom he'd repelled and that he felt so self-conscious about his appearance that he wanted the fresh clothes before consulting the police. He didn't think the clerk had bought the story. There was no reason it should have been bought—why purchase a pair of slacks when you're carrying luggage, one piece of which is clearly a suit bag? In the taxicab he'd taken after leaving the store, Frost had changed out of his suitcoat and into a blue denim jeans jacket. His shoulder rig and the Browning High Power were wrapped up in his old pants. He'd changed taxicabs twice more; before he caught the last one he'd ditched the eye patch over his left eye and replaced it with dark, big-lensed aviator-style sunglasses.

As Frost exited the taxicab now, he stretched, and snapping up the collar on his denim jacket, he reached back inside the taxi for his luggage. He'd shifted the shoulder rig, still wrapped inside the old trousers, into the SWAT bag; the Browning High Power nestled in his trouser band slightly behind his left hip bone, butt forward.

"You sure this is where you wanted to go, mister?"

Frost looked back at the cabdriver. "Yeah—I think so." He handed the man a twenty and, waiting for his change, looked down the narrow, dirt road ahead of him leading off the highway.

"I can drive you in there if you want," the driver volunteered.

Frost absent-mindedly shook his head, saying, "No—thanks anyway."

He stood by the side of the highway, staring up the dirt road as the taxi moved off. The sign by the dirt road read BLUEBOY NURSERY. It had to be the right place, he thought. When Deacon had written the name of the place down on the matchbook, Frost hadn't thought to ask anything about it—and Blueboy Nursery was definitely not the kind of nursery where they had little kids. On the last cab drive, Frost had mentally reviewed the only nursery rhyme he knew: Little Boy Blue, come blow your kazoo; The sheep's in the meadow; The cow's in there, too. Where's the little boy who's watching the sheep? Behind the haystack, kissin' Bo-Peep.

"All for nothing," he smiled, whispering to himself. Blueboy Nursery didn't raise children—it raised Christmas trees, or at least that was what the small print said on the sign.

Frost shouldered his baggage and started walking up the dirt road, his sixty-five-dollar shoes still squishing and wet from the stream under the bridge near the hospital. He'd elected to walk up the road rather than use the taxicab. If somehow the information on where Jessica Pace was hiding had been pried out of Andy Deacon, Frost felt he stood a better chance in a trap if he could take to the woods rather than be stuck in a vehicle.

More important than retrieving his clothes back at the hospital had been retrieving his gear—and now the Interdynamics KG-9 9-mm assault pistol, the bulk of the spare magazines for the Browning, and the big German MkII were secure. If he did successfully link up with Jessica Pace and they started the cross-country run for Washington, in light of the opposition he'd encountered so far, Frost decided he'd need all the firepower he could get. He wished for an assault rifle, but his CAR-15 was locked away back in Indiana and there was no way to obtain one legally in California—California was hardly contiguous to South Bend. He smiled. There were always ways of obtaining almost anything through other than legal means, but for the moment at least Frost had no desire to have a federal weapons charge against him so he'd content himself with his existing ordnance.

He reached a small bend in the steep dirt road and turned it, then stopped. It reassured him to hear the sounds of birds in the trees flanking the road—had there been men in the woods waiting to ambush him, the birds would have gone and there'd be total silence. He remembered once in Vietnam laying an ambush for a high-ranking V.C. officer and the patrol escorting the man. It had been important to capture the officer alive and well for later interrogation. To avoid alerting the patrol Frost had borrowed a cassette tape recorder, and prior to going out into the jungle, left the machine running and recorded forty-five minutes' worth of jungle animal and bird noises. In addition to the regular arms and equipment when Frost had led his men out on the ambush, he'd carried the recorder and two sets of stereo speakers a guy in the motor pool had rigged to work with a portable battery-operated recorder. The V.C. patrol had walked blissfully into the ambush, not suspecting men were hiding in the jungle because the jungle noises had been right. Frost smiled to himself, wondering if some clever FBI or CIA man was sitting off in the trees right now, playing a cassette recording. He hoped not.

Frost started walking again, up the road and

toward the small two-story house and wide, low garage beside it. Behind the house and garage Frost could see the nearest of several greenhouses, long, low, glass-enclosed structures. He knew little about plants he realized, but decided it was safe to assume the Blueboy Nursery people grew their trees from seedlings; hence the greenhouses.

Frost walked to the base of the front-porch steps and then started up, leaving his cases on the front-porch floor and walking the few steps to the front door. He saw no doorbell, so he knocked, and lit a Camel in the blue-yellow flame of his battered Zippo, inhaling the smoke deeply into his lungs as he waited. He squinted skyward, despite his dark glasses. The sun was strong, and a pleasantly cool breeze blew against his face from the west.

He turned back to the door, starting to knock again.

His hand froze as the screen door opened outward toward him.

Frost made a smile appear on his face, but held his cigarette cupped in his right hand between his first finger and thumb, ready to be snapped into the face of the person at the door if need be, to buy him a split second to get to his gun.

"Yes—can I help you?"

"Yes, Ma'am," Frost told the housedress-clad woman. He guessed her age at somewhere in the middle to late fifties; she was somewhat on the chubby side, but not unpleasantly so, with short gray hair carefully combed framing her full face and dark-rimmed glasses balanced precariously on her nose. "I am a friend of Andy Deacon. You know he's in the hospital."

"Yes—I'd read about it in the papers," the old woman cooed.

"Well, I understand Andy was supposed to come here and pick up some valuable old books he was interested in acquiring." Frost always felt stupid using code phrases and recognition signals.

"Books?"

"Yes—a nineteenth-century Canadian imprint of one of Mark Twain's works, I believe—the title escapes me." Frost waited—now the woman was supposed to tell him the title.

"*Old Times on the Mississippi*, wasn't it?"

Frost smiled at the woman, saying, "I'm glad that's over."

"Andrew said that if he couldn't make it he'd send someone and tell him what to say. Is Andrew going to be all right?"

"Yes, ma'am—I think so," Frost told her honestly.

"He's my nephew—a good boy, really." She smiled.

"Yes, ma'am—can I see Jessica Pace?"

"She's out back in the greenhouses—I think greenhouse B with the Georgia pines."

The woman smiled and as Frost started to turn away, he turned back, saying, "Can I just leave my things here?"

"You can put them inside the door if you'd like."

"Fine," Frost told her, as he caught up his baggage and started for the door.

"Just inside here, young man," the woman cooed.

"Yes, ma'am." Frost smiled back, stepping inside the small hallway, realizing as he did it that something was wrong, that he was being stupid. He started to let go of the baggage, to straighten up, to snatch at the Browning High Power in his trouser band, when he felt—heard—movement behind him and tried to spin around on the balls of his feet; his right hand touched the butt of the Browning.

It wasn't actually pain, but a dullness; then bright floaters over his eye and a burst of light. Frost could faintly make out the worn Oriental rug smashing up toward his face as the blackness washed over him. . . .

Frost opened his eye, but all he could see was diffused light, no images. There was a sack or maybe a pillowcase over his head—he couldn't be sure. He tried to move, but his hands were bound together behind him at the wrists and he was naked—he could feel the coldness of a stone floor under him. He tried moving again, this time discovering his ankles were tied as well and that when he moved his ankles there was pressure around his neck—some sort of noose.

"You awake?"

It was a woman's voice—he mentally bet with himself it was Jessica Pace.

"I said, you awake?"

"You get your butt over here and untie me—right now," Frost snapped.

"Shut up," and Frost felt something hard and round pressing against the front of his forehead. "Know what that is?"

"A gun—do I win the prize?" Frost rasped angrily.

"*Your* gun—the Browning. Now you keep quiet and only answer the questions I ask—try moving, try telling me something I didn't ask about and you get this," the voice snarled—and the muzzle of the Browning ground into his forehead.

"Now—Andy Deacon sent you—what's your name?"

"You read my wallet," Frost snapped.

"What's your name?" The voice was rising, angry-sounding, and he could feel the muzzle of his gun twisting hard against his forehead.

"Frost—Hank Frost—you know that, damn it!"

"What did Deacon tell you?"

"Who are you?" Frost asked.

This time the muzzle of the pistol moved away from him. He could feel its absence, then feel it hammer into his stomach. His back arched and his legs stretched and he felt the noose tightening around his neck.

"Now we'll try again," he heard the voice say, the words sounding as though they were being spit out between clenched teeth.

"What?" Frost choked.

"What did Deacon tell you?"

Frost mentally shrugged, trying to ease the tension of the noose around his neck as he spoke, recounting what Deacon had told him in the hospital room, the recognition signal to the old woman—Deacon's supposed aunt—everything. Finally, after what seemed to him like an eternity, the woman asked another question.

"What are your plans?"

"Are you Jessica Pace?" Frost asked back.

The muzzle of the pistol left his forehead and he braced for another shot to the stomach. Instead, he felt something—a hand—at the top of his head, felt the sack or pillowcase moving; he almost choked as the thing caught in the noose around his neck. The thing covering his head—it was a pillowcase—was pulled up, and he squinted against the light.

The woman had long, straight dark-red hair, brown eyes, and a pale complexion. She looked tall—at least from where Frost lay on the floor. Deacon had described her to him and as far as Frost could tell, this was the woman. His Browning was in her right fist and there was a smaller, medium-frame automatic shoved into the beltless waistband of the faded blue jeans she wore.

"Jessica Pace?"

"Yeah," the woman answered emotionlessly. "Sorry about having to cold-cock you, pal," she added.

"Aww, listen—I can understand your wanting to be on the cautious side." Frost smiled.

"Then no hard feelings?" The woman smiled.

"Hey—listen, just get me untied, huh?" Frost told her.

She bent down to his ankles, using a pair of household shears to cut the clothesline binding his feet together. Almost immediately, the pressure around his neck and throat eased, the tension on the noose around it relaxed.

She pulled the pillowcase all the way off; then held the scissors close to his throat—too close, he thought—and snipped the noose. She turned him around on the floor and cut the ropes around his wrists. "There—why don't you take a stretch?"

"Good idea," Frost said cheerfully. He noticed the Browning in her hand had the safety on, the hammer cocked. Frost swept his left leg around and up, catching Jessica Pace behind the knees, making them buckle. His hands reached up, grabbing for the High Power, his left thumb easing between the cocked hammer and the frame to prevent the pistol from going off. His right hand whipped down, snatching the blued medium-frame automatic from her pants as she started to fall face-first to the floor.

The girl came out of it in a roll, starting for him, but Frost was already on his feet, one pistol in each hand. "Why the routine?" Frost snarled.

"I had to be sure—"

"Why the hell you take my clothes, tie me—"

"I had to search you first, damn it. This is the big league, Captain Frost—you know that as well as I do. I heard about the hospital thing on a radio broadcast; then on the next broadcast there wasn't a word about it—the government put the lid on it. They don't want local cops arresting you or me—they want to get us and kill us!"

"Where are my clothes?"

"Over there in a heap in the corner," the woman half-shouted, pointing with her right hand.

Frost glanced down to the little medium-frame automatic—there was a movie-style silencer on it, long, thin, sausage-shaped. The gun was a Walther PPK 9-mm short; .380 in the U.S. Frost started across the room toward his clothes, setting the guns down on a workbench. The building they were in was apparently a garage.

"You cool now, Captain Frost?" the woman went on, behind him.

Frost pulled up his pants and zipped them. He looked down at his bare feet. Frost turned around toward her, his right hand sailing out ahead of him, the palm of his hand open, his knuckles backhanding into Jessica Pace's right cheek. She screamed, a sharp, little scream, her head snapping back, her body collapsing away from him, landing in a heap on the floor by his feet. She pushed herself up on her hands, her legs splayed out, the right side of her face darkening and red.

"Now I'm cool," Frost told her. Not bothering with his socks, he stuck his feet into his sixty-five-dollar shoes, caught up his clothes and guns, and started for the side door.

"You bastard," he heard her muttering behind him.

Frost turned and looked back at her, his hand on the knob, the door half-opened inward. "Yeah, well—if you make it to Washington alive, kid—it's this bastard that's gonna be gettin' you there!"

The one-eyed man walked through the doorway, slamming the door closed behind him—it was the only way not to hear her cursing at him. . . .

There was a healthy bruise where he'd backhanded her across the face and Frost studied it for a moment as Andrew Deacon's aunt brought two cups of coffee and set them on the white wooden kitchen table on the screened-in back porch, then left. "We can't leave right away, Frost," the woman said flatly to him.

66

"Why—we've—"

"The car won't be back until tomorrow morning—that's why. If you want to haul that trailer with us because you think it'll make us look less conspicuous, then we need the big Ford. Period!"

"All right," Frost acquiesced; "then we leave in the morning." He looked past her, not liking her, watching the sunset.

"And why the hell you wanna go south . . . we'd be better off—"

"I know the southerly route pretty well," Frost told her, his own voice sounding angry and tired to him. "If we get spotted—*when* we get spotted—I want to know my ground pretty well. You're just the luggage on this trip—I'm the transporter. Remember that."

"Would you young people like to come in for dinner now?"

Frost turned and stared toward the doorway. It was Andy Deacon's aunt, standing there, smiling. "Sure," he said, shrugging his shoulders and smiling at the woman. "Ahh," and he looked at Jessica Pace. "What's that expression about the condemned man and the hearty meal?"

Frost didn't wait for an answer.

The second floor of the house was really an apartment separate from the first floor—the woman, Deacon's aunt Beatrice, had mentioned at dinner that her daughter had lived upstairs until she'd married and moved out. Frost had met Deacon's uncle, too—Morris Carruthers—who had joined them midway through the meal, and after introductions, had

67

confirmed that the 1978 Ford LTD with the hitch would be back in service by midmorning. Finally, Frost could no longer bear the suspense and had asked Deacon's aunt just how much she knew about Jessica Pace, and about what her nephew Andy had been up to. The woman was amazingly, almost ludicrously candid in her reply, Frost remembered. "Andy had told us Miss Pace was on the lam from the feds because some Commie moles had worked their way into the bureau and the company and were out to waste her."

Frost, standing under the shower spray, laughed thinking about the old woman; laughed in spite of himself, in spite of the fact that each second he spent anywhere near Jessica Pace upped immeasurably his chances of dying at an early age.

He turned the water to straight cold and stood under it for a while. Each moment he spent near Jessica also made it that much more likely that he'd get into a shoot-out with CIA and FBI people. The thought of shooting it out with good men simply out to protect national security because they'd been told to do that made his skin crawl, despite the stinging cold spray under which he stood.

"Damn it," Frost muttered, then turned down the water and shut off the faucet, stepping out of the shower and staring at himself in the mirror. Frost looked at the scar where his left eye had been. Soon, almost a decade would have passed since he'd lost it. He laughed at the face that stared back at him—his own. He'd lost an eye, but compensated for it. Now he'd lost Bess—there was no compensating for that. While she'd been alive, it hadn't bothered him—as much as it should have at any event—to be with other women. If their marriage had gone as planned, it would have been different, he told himself. And he knew that there'd be other women now—but it was still no compensation.

Frost, still naked from the shower, walked across the bedroom floor and sat on the edge of the bed. When he strained, he could hear the night sounds through the half-open screened window. He stood up, walked to the window and stared out into the night. Somewhere out there, he thought—

Frost wheeled, his left hand—closer—reaching out to the Metalifed Browning High Power on the dresser, thumbing back the hammer to full stand.

"Relax—God, you're jumpy." Jessica Pace laughed.

"You always walk in on people?" Frost rasped, lowering the Browning's hammer and setting the gun on the dresser.

"Seems like I always see you without your clothes on."

"That should be my line," Frost told her.

"You know, nobody's socked me around—no man anyway—since I knew this guy in high school."

"I'm sorry," Frost said emotionlessly. "You like being socked around?"

"It depends on who and why—you had it coming."

"No," Frost started to laugh. "*You* had it coming."

"Anyway," she said, her fingers drifting up to the front of the white blouse she wore, starting to unbutton it. "I figured I'd come and make a peace offering."

"Is that a double entendre?" Frost asked her.

"If you want it to be. I mean, sooner or later, traveling across the country together and all, I guess I figure it's inevitable. Don't you?"

"Well," Frost began, "if you want an honest answer—"

"Did I say that?" She smiled, the blouse all the way open now. She shrugged it off and onto the floor. She started walking toward him, across the few yards that separated them, her hands behind her back; then the bra she wore slipped forward, the straps coming from her shoulders. She tossed it onto the floor.

"I know," she smiled. "They're little."

"I'll get out the calipers," Frost cracked. "Have you tried acne medicine?"

"You don't like me, do you?"

"Did I say that?" Frost smiled.

"Well—do you want me?"

Frost looked at her a moment. "Will it hurt your feelings?"

"I'll be crushed."

"No—this way you'll be—" Frost took her in his arms, his mouth going down on hers. Somehow, he found himself having gotten her near enough to the bed that they fell onto it, the woman—Jessica Pace—still holding him, her arms around his neck. Maybe it was because it *was* inevitable, Frost reflected for a moment, looking at her. Maybe, then again, it was because of a lot of things. . . .

Chapter Five

"Aagh!" Frost looked at the trailer hitch and decided that if he kicked it with his left foot the next time, he'd probably hurt his left big toe. "What—you gotta be an engineer to put this thing together with the car or what?"

He stepped back, staring alternately at the trailer tongue and the grease on his hands, trying to figure out how you got the little ball on the car's trailer hitch to get inside the little socket on the trailer tongue. He was mentally debating if it would be better to trust to staying in motels after all. "If God had meant man to drag his house behind him wherever he went, he would have—"

"What are you talking about?" Jessica Pace asked, suddenly there besides him.

"Ohh," Frost said, turning to look at her, "nothing at all—just trying to remember the words of an old song, that's all." He smiled.

"Ahh—an old song, hmm? Why are you standing here staring at the trailer rather than hitching it?"

"Admiring the workmanship," he told her. "All the wonderful craftsmanship that goes into these things—golly, whiz!"

"Bullshit!"

"Tsk, tsk," Frost told her. "I would never have thought a lady such as yourself would have even known such a word."

"So—go hitch the trailer then."

"Do you know how to hitch a trailer?" Frost asked brightly.

"I haven't done it in years," she told him.

"Well—listen," Frost began. "Just in case something happens and you should need to know how to do it, I think it'd be wise for you to try it now—you know, rather than do it in an emergency and mess it up."

"You're puttin' me on!"

"Naw," Frost drawled.

"You serious?"

"Yeah," Frost said, keeping his face as straight as he could. "I think you need the practice. I'll watch and if you're starting to do anything wrong, I'll help you out. Then we'll both be competent in trailer-hitching just in case the need arises for you to do it. Go on."

"You wanna jockey the car around?"

"Well, I would," Frost told her, "but I think even though it might be simpler if we did it together, you know—better you learn how to do it yourself, you know—relearn, so to speak."

"Frost—are you—"

"Now go on—do it. I wanna make sure you can do it as well as I can. Never know what might happen," and Frost gestured dramatically to his side, "out there on the trail."

She reached up and gently swung his arm in the other direction. "Out there, Frost, is west—if we take the trailer out there, we sink. It's out *there* that the trail is—east."

"Just testing," he told her. It wasn't his fault, he reassured himself, that he'd missed the sunrise that morning.

He watched as Jessica—disgust written all over her face—climbed behind the wheel of the LTD and—expertly, Frost thought—jockeyed the full-sized car to within two inches of the trailer tongue and slightly off center from it. She got out, sneering at him, then worked something that he decided was a jack of some sort. The front of the trailer miraculously seemed to be rising. She took something that he instantly identified as a big cotter pin out of the socket on the trailer tongue, worked some kind of lever and got back into the car, inching it forward, then back, then getting out again, checking the spacing between the hitch and the receptacle on the trailer tongue. "You know, Hank, you could help me."

"Hey—listen, you're doin' just great. I'm impressed." He wasn't lying, he decided.

Another turn at the wheel got the ball under the socket, then with ridiculous ease, she lowered the trailer tongue down over the ball on the car hitch—and the two mated perfectly!

Frost thought, They must teach you a great many mysteries in spy school!

Satisfied that he'd never be able to hitch a trailer in a thousand years, he applauded Jessica's efforts, telling her that he thought that the next few times they hitched and unhitched, she should do it—she could use the practice, he thought. Before she could answer him, he started back up to the house to wash his hands—and heal his pride, he realized. . . .

Frost had never seen the inside of a trailer before, either. He had been amazed. There was a shower, a stove, an oven, beds, tables, a kitchen sink, even—he decided it was vastly better than his apartment. There were even windows.

He pondered this as he stood for the last time on the front porch of Deacon's aunt and uncle's house. Trailering would be a new experience for him. Bess had once told him—

He burned his fingers on the stub of the cigarette in his hand and snapped it down into the dirt driveway. He started down the steps, shooting a final wave to Deacon's aunt and uncle, heading toward the car. Jessica was already standing beside it.

"Are you ready—finally?"

"What do you mean—'finally'?"

"I mean finally—if we take this long every time we—"

"You're a nag—you know that?" Frost told the girl.

"Are you going to drive?"

Frost stopped in midstride, feeling his face brightening. "Now that you mention it, I think it wouldn't be a bad idea—"

She cut him off. ". . . For me to get the practice—just in case?"

"Right." Frost smiled. Before she could say anything, he walked around the front of the car and let himself in on the passenger side. As soon as she touched her foot to the gas pedal, he knew he'd made a mistake.

"Harrowing." Frost stared out the window, watching the mountains disappear in the distance behind them in the reflection of the big west-coast mirror on the right fender.

"What did you say?"

"Harrowing," Frost answered calmly, looking at Jessica Pace, then looking away—he realized she was looking at him instead of the road.

"What do you mean harrowing? I mean, what a chicken shit you are!"

"You should have been sitting where I was sitting," Frost said, keeping his voice calm, trying to light a cigarette despite his shaking hands.

"What do you mean?"

"I mean—lady, did you see how close you were to those drops back there? And that trailer swinging and swaying after the car—God!"

"If you don't like the way I drive—" She stopped talking as she cut the wheel left pulling the moving car off the shoulder, the trailer swaying behind the car again. "—Then you can—" Frost turned and looked at her, saw her looking at him, then saw that they were crossing over into the oncoming lanes.

"Look out!"

She cut the wheel right, the trailer swaying again; Frost started to get a sick feeling in his stomach. "All right—stop the car. Now!"

She did, and Frost almost smacked his head against the dashboard. "God, woman!"

He ran around to the front of the car, thinking better of it—what if she hadn't set the parking brake? He climbed in behind the wheel, almost injuring himself, forgetting she had the seat forward.

Frost adjusted the seat, released the emergency brake, and started to move the selector into drive. "Sucker," she snapped.

Frost looked at her. "What?"

"I suckered you good, Hank—ha!"

"You—"

"I not only went through CIA's counterterrorist driving course, I went through the same thing for the KGB—and I taught regular driving when I was working my way through graduate school. It supported my habit out at the drag strip. I used to race class—"

Frost cracked, "You—"

"Ha!"

"What the hell is this thing?" Frost pointed to a brown box with a blinking red light mounted near the base of the steering wheel.

"It's an electric trailer brake—expert."

"Ohh." Frost lit a cigarette and rolled down the window, staring into the rear-view mirror—all he could see was the trailer behind him. It was, he decided, going to be a long drive to Phoenix. . . .

Frost sat at the larger of the two tables in the trailer, the one forward by the awninged front window. Jessica Pace was cooking something that the one-eyed man grudgingly admitted smelled good. But most of his attention was on the small, black-and-white portable television they'd brought along. The news was almost over. He stood up, shut off the set, and walked the few steps to the screen door, feeling the evening cool, listening to the night noises. There had been nothing on the news about the manhunt for himself and the girl, nothing about the affair at the hospital. The absence of coverage confirmed for him the broadness of the conspiracy which they were up against—news blackouts weren't easy to come by.

"Did you say something?"

Frost turned around, looking at Jessica Pace for a long moment, then only shook his head, no. She turned back to the stove and he studied her back. She had changed from the blue jeans she'd worn—changed into something that was apparently a sun dress, but wore a heavy coat sweater over it. She was pretty, he decided, watching her move her head. The red hair undulated as she did, almost like a living thing pressed against her back. He felt a smile raise the corners of his mouth. With the size and caliber of the opposition, he wondered just how long either of them would remain a living thing. . . .

Chapter Six

"Pull over at the rest area—I can use the john in the trailer," Jessica Pace said. Frost was not watching her, his fists were wrapped so tightly around the Ford's steering wheel that his knuckles were white. He'd decided that in another day or so of driving he might get the hang of hauling a trailer—at least not feel so terribly nervous about it.

"What did you say?" Frost asked her, having only half-registered her comment.

"I said I wanna go to the bathroom, Hank. Pull over into the rest area up there before we miss it, so I can use the—"

"Ohh," Frost began. "Right—yeah," and he craned his neck far to the right trying to get a better look in the right-hand west-coast mirror—just in case anything was coming up along the shoulder, he told himself.

"Maybe it's because you only got one eye, Hank," Jessica told him.

"What is?"

"The problems you're having with the trailer."

"What's one eye got to do with it?"

"Cuts down your field of vision—right?"

"So?" Frost snapped, by now tired of the conversation.

"So—you feel less secure with the trailer behind you because you subconsciously think you're missing something you should be able to see but can't see."

"Nuts," he told her, putting on the directional signal and starting to edge slightly into the right-hand lane; the exit for the rest area was coming up.

"No—we're subject to a great many subconscious stresses. I didn't know if you knew that or not."

"You into horoscopes, too?"

"I'm serious," she insisted.

Frost shot a glance toward her, almost losing the trailer, he thought, then riveted his stare ahead of the car again. "I know you're serious—that's the problem. Why don't you look at the map or something?"

"No—I told you, I gotta go to the bathroom."

"You can't read when you gotta—?"

"No. I know where we are—you're just trying to tell me to shut up."

"You got it, kid." Frost smiled. He almost lost the trailer again, he felt, cutting the wheel ever so slightly right and aiming the car and the trailer up into the exit.

"We're in New Mexico—and if we could go a little faster than that lousy fifty-five you've been doin', we'd get into El Paso before the owls go to sleep, too."

"Well—if you don't like the way I'm drivin', then I can fix that really easy," Frost told her.

"No—you just drive away and meander along—I'll go to sleep."

"Like hell you will," Frost answered.

Frost eyed the sign telling cars pulling trailers to pull right in the rest-area parking lot. He was pleased to find the lot relatively empty with a clear path to a drive-through space. He started cutting the wheel—on time for once—and eased the big LTD through the space.

There was a loud sigh from Jessica Pace on the seat beside him. " 'Bout time—the old kidneys were about to scream, baby." She laughed.

She started to get out of the car, but Frost reached across and grabbed her left arm. "I don't know how to tell you this," he began, "but there's kidding and then there's kidding. I like a girl with a sense of humor—I really do. But I don't like grossness in a man, let alone a woman—why don't you stop trying to be a bad caricature of one of the boys, huh?"

Her eyes bored into his but Frost's right eye never wavered. His voice low, he said, "We've got a long way to go yet. I know that what you've got under all

80

that red hair is really important, that you're under a lot of pressure—the whole nine yards. But a couple thousand miles more of the way it is now and I promise you, after you spill what you know to the President, I'm gonna clip ya right in the teeth.'' She didn't say anything, just shook his hand off her left forearm and started out through the passenger door.

Frost cut the ignition and dropped the keys into his pocket. He got a Camel from a half-crushed packet in his jeans jacket, and lit it with his battered Zippo. Then he stared at the half-transparent reflection of his face in the tinted glass of the windshield. He decided he missed Bess even more than he'd realized, talking the way he had to Jessica Pace. If she wanted to be the way she was, she had every right to be. He wondered then, for the billionth time, he decided, if Bess had died just because violence seemed to be attracted to him and she had gotten caught up in it? He'd heard or seen the phrase in countless movies and books, but somehow, despite its triteness, it seemed to capture the essence of the thing—wallowing in self-pity. He'd been doing that. Jessica Pace would never have cold-cocked him that day back at Deacon's aunt's house; he would have handled the thing at the hospital less sloppily. . . . He promised himself something. There had been no leads, no way to trace out the killers, the terrorists, the bombers—whatever you called them. But as soon as the thing with Jessica Pace was over, he would go back to Europe and spend the rest of his life—and every dime he had if need be—to find the person most directly responsible for Bess being killed. He felt the Camel burning the flesh of his fingers, looked at it a moment, then snapped it out the open car window. To find that person was the only way he'd ever exorcise what was in him. The feelings for Bess, the grief that she was gone from him—all of that would never leave, he knew. But at least if he got her—

"Hank!"

Frost turned and stared across the front seat. Jessica Pace, standing by the open passenger door, looked back at him.

"What—what do you want?" he asked her, his voice sounding lifeless to him.

"You see those guys—that car over there?"

'What—?" Frost followed her stare, past him and out the open window at his side.

It was a green sedan that seemed identical to the one that had followed him from the airport in Los Angeles, the one he'd forced the FBI man/cabdriver to lose. There were two men, one inside it and the other walking from it, but from the distance Frost couldn't see faces. He realized, too, that there was no reason to suppose he would have recognized the faces anyway. "Jessica," he snapped, "reach over into the rear seat—that small black case. Take the Bushnells out of it and try to see if you recognize any faces."

"They'll see!" she blurted out. "They'll know we're watching them."

"You let me worry about that. If they're straight, they'll just think we're rude. If they're after our tails, they'll at least know we're onto them. Just do as I say, huh?" Frost lit another cigarette. He snatched the map from the glove compartment, checking the road ahead as well as the standard gas-station map allowed. The way the road wound, there were either mountains or canyons, he assumed.

"It's Boronovitch—he's a KGB man," Jessica half-gasped.

Frost glanced at the girl, then back through the window, tossing the map onto the back seat. "Boronovitch, huh? With a name like that I'd have sworn he was Irish. Get all the way in and get that door closed," he snapped.

"What are you going to—?"

"The one guy's out over at that phone now, right? Trying to call—shaking the coin return? Probably out of order. If he's using a phone, means he doesn't have a radio, so let's ditch them before he finds a phone that works."

"What are you—?" She interrupted herself, slamming the door closed.

"Lock it," Frost commanded, starting to fumble his seat belt into position. "And buckle up, kid!"

"You aren't—"

"Yeah!"

"The way you drive? And with this trailer? Let me—"

"Keep that .380 peashooter handy, huh?" Frost glanced behind him—then swore at himself. All he could see was the trailer. He peered into the side-view mirrors, turned the key, and checked the gas gauge—almost full. A thought flashed across his mind—why hadn't Jessica Pace used the bathroom at the service station twenty miles back up the road? Or why hadn't she just walked back into the camper trailer then while he'd been filling up? Why the rest area—? He could have stopped anywhere on the road shoulder and she could have gotten out and used the bathroom in the trailer. Frost looked out the open driver's window, spitting his Camel onto the pavement as he glanced toward the green car and started the engine of his own car. He shouted out the window, "Hey—you guys in the green car—"

The one coming back from the phone kiosk turned, looking across the parking lot at him. Frost assumed it was the one she'd called Boronovitch—didn't look Russian, though, Frost thought. "Hey!"

The man looked squarely back at Frost and Frost shouted, "Wanna play bumper tag, asshole!" Frost didn't wait for an answer, but hauled the stick into drive and stomped down on the gas pedal. The car lurched as it dragged the trailer behind it, then roared forward along the level parking area surface. Frost cut across the unoccupied, neatly painted parking spots, aiming the hood ornament of the LTD toward the rest-area exit ramp. He shot a glance into the left-hand side-view mirror. The green car was already moving slowly, and the man he'd shouted to was jumping into it and swinging the door closed. There was a screech of tires and Frost could see the green car shoot forward. He felt the corners of his mouth raising into a smile. He was feeling alive again. He wondered, half to himself, if he were crazy—did he like this stuff?

He cut the wheel too hard right and veered onto the exit ramp, the trailer fishtailing behind him. His left hand reached down to work manually the electric trailer brake and his right foot hammered down the gas pedal to drag the trailer straight. He released the trailer brake; as he flicked the directional signal on with his left hand and glanced into the side-view, the car suddenly seemed to lurch ahead. There was a truck, a massive eighteen-wheeler moving van, roaring up on his left; its screeching air horns were deafening.

Frost hammered down harder on the gas pedal. The truck pulled left into the passing lane, while Frost hugged the trailer onto the right shoulder. As the truck shot past, the slipstream of the massive moving van sucked at the camper Frost pulled behind the LTD. In the mirror behind him Frost could now see the green car as well, and an object—long and thin—protruding from the passenger-side front window—a gun?

Frost worked the trailer brake, trying to stop the sway behind him, as he cut the Ford's steering wheel hard left and off the shoulder, back onto the pavement. The green car was coming up beside them. There was a shot, then a second and a third—a handgun Frost guessed. He cut the wheel hard right. The trailer camper's rear end swayed left, and the green car accelerated away onto the opposite shoulder. Frost cut the wheel back left; the trailer swayed behind them as Jessica Pace sucked in her breath so hard it sounded like a scream. Frost edged the trailer left, intentionally swaying the trailer behind the Ford, keeping the green car blocked behind them. There was another shot, and Frost heard the sound of glass shattering. He glanced to his right and there was a bullet hole spider-webbed across the west-coast mirror on the LTD's right front fender.

"Frost! There's—"

There was another shot and Frost lost the rest of her words, feeling a bumping and lurching—the green car was right behind the trailer bumper, he realized. He craned his neck toward the center of the front seat to get a better angle out of the left-side west-coast mirror. He closed his eye, blinking it, then stared. There was a man moving on the hood of the green car. Frost tried to accelerate, the Ford and the trailer lurching ahead too little—they were entering a grade. Frost glanced to his right—the world was dropping off there, a steep drop then a void growing there beyond the road. He felt the impact again against the back of the trailer, the steering wheel of the big Ford wrenching under his hands.

"Frost—one of them's climbing onto the trailer!"

"If he shoots and gets me, we'll go over the edge—but so will he. . . . Is it that important? To die for it?"

Chapter Six

He glanced to his right, his eye catching the girl's eyes. Her voice sounded strangely sober to him. "Yes—yes, Hank, it is."

Frost glanced to his left—he could barely see part of the KGB man's body in the mirror now; then it vanished. The man was climbing up the ladder at the back of the camper, then would climb up onto the luggage rack on the camper roof, then cross to the front of the camper. He could crouch there, lie down there—whatever, Frost thought—and potshot Frost behind the wheel.

"Here—I'm getting out—slide over here and

catch the wheel—"

"Getting out!"

"I gotta stop that son of a—" The trailer lurched again, the green car apparently crowding it. Frost's right foot was flat against the floorboards now, the trailer and car doing fifty if the speedometer read right. "Damn," he rasped. Jessica Pace undid her seatbelt, starting across the seat toward him. Frost edged up, already pushing the driver's side door open with his left hand, getting his rear end up from the seat, but keeping his right foot on the gas—like a mechanic starting a car without activating the seatbelt buzzer. His right hand was clamped like a vise on the left side of the steering wheel, the Ford and the trailer it pulled swaying toward the soft gravel shoulder to their right, toward the drop-off beyond it. "Hurry—damn it," he shouted, barely able to hear his own voice over the wind's slipstream.

Jessica Pace was in position behind the wheel now—he heard her shouting, "You'll be killed, Frost—killed!"

Frost hated people who showed their brains by stating the obvious. He felt the pressure of her hands on the wheel—he could no longer see it, his head above the level of the LTD's roofline; his neck twisted, craning back, looking for some sign the KGB gunman had made it to the top of the trailer.

Frost let go of the wheel, pushing himself up with his hands, his feet—hearing Jessica Pace shouting at him. He guessed he'd kicked her. Frost stretched out his hands, spread-eagling the upper half of his body on the blue vinyl roof, then hauling his legs after him. He glanced up to the trailer roof, thinking he'd seen the silhouette of a hand there. "Dummy," he rasped. He could have crawled out the back door, straight onto the trunk lid instead of crossing the roof. "Damn it," he shouted into the wind around him, inching back across the roof of the big Ford, the wind blowing his hair down into his eye. He pushed his right hand back to get the hair from his forehead, then inched along. His hands were on the chrome molding strip where the roofline met the rear window. He edged his body around, getting onto his back, dropping his legs, feeling with his feet for the trunk lid somewhere beneath them. There was something solid and he let himself slide forward, his rear end skidding down along the rear-window glass. His feet were slipping off the trunk lid—he glanced down. The pavement below was a blur, and to his right was the drop-off into some canyon—he didn't want to die in someplace he didn't know the name of. His hands spread-eagled on his sides, the fingers splayed—and the slipping of his feet stopped. He pulled his feet toward him, tucking them under him, already eying the propane gas canisters and the trailer tongue just forward of them. He'd have to jump, he realized.

Frost edged his feet down onto the rear bumper of the LTD, forcing himself into a standing position, his hands balanced behind him on the trunk lid. "Why am I doing this!" he screamed into the wind that shoved at him, that seemed to be trying to make him lose his balance.

Snapping his hands and arms ahead of him like a broad jumper, he dived toward the trailer tongue, his hands reaching out, grabbing at the plastic awning covering the trailer's front window. His left foot slipped between the trailer tongue and the gas canisters. His fingers now started to slip, the nails of his left hand scratching along the plastic awning. He brought his left knee up and pushed against the gas canisters, then fought his way to his feet, glancing above him—the KGB gunman would be there. Frost felt it. There was no way to the top of the trailer from where he stood; the door of the trailer was on the right-hand side, his left, and there were louvered windows there—handholds, perhaps. He edged both feet onto the right side of the trailer tongue, reaching around the trailer body with his left hand, finding the empty awning rail there; his fingers gouged against it as he shifted his weight. There was a small fender—plastic-looking—that was more of a rock guard, over the right front wheel of the trailer. Frost edged his left foot onto it. As his foot slipped, the fingers of his left hand locked onto the awning track. He felt himself screaming from the pain in his hand, but in the wind his voice was lost to his hearing. He moved his left foot up again, against the meager purchase of the fender, tested his weight against it, and swung his right foot off the trailer tongue and onto the fender. Both hands now grasped the tiny awning rail above him. Frost reached out with his left hand grabbing for the aluminum window frame, his fingers pushing against it, searching blindly for a hold there. Frost looked down—the handle for the trailer door was at his belt line, not really a handle at all, but a cavity into which you reached your hand to pull open the door handle recessed into it. Would the toe of his left shoe fit there?

Frost edged his left foot off the fender, up to waist level, ahead of him, and out, cramming the toe of his left shoe into the cavity beside the door handle. The fingers of his right hand still clutched the awning rail; his left hand was on the window frame. He shifted his weight onto the left foot, then pushed up with his left hand. The nails of his right hand felt as though they were being pulled from his fingertips as he clung to the awning rail. He let go, thrusting his right hand up toward the luggage rack on top of the trailer. His fist locked onto it; then he released his left hand. His left fist locked beside the right on the luggage rack. He started to push himself up with his left foot, looking up. The one-eyed man snapped his head back as a foot flew toward his face. Both his feet swayed in empty air space below him; his wrists and fingers burned with the sudden pressure of his full weight.

It was the KGB gunman whose foot flashed out toward his hands now. Frost felt the impact, his right hand suddenly going numb, his fingers slipping, his full weight hanging from the side of the trailer—the abyss to his right and below him. His left fist locked on the luggage rack. Frost swung himself around, forward, his chest slamming against the side of the trailer. His right hand flashed up, though he didn't know if his fingers there still worked enough to grab hold. He could see the foot coming again; his right eye involuntarily closed. Frost felt the kick, felt the fingers of his right hand loosening from the luggage rack above him. The trailer swayed suddenly, toward the drop; gravel sprayed up toward Frost's face, pelting his skin and the skin of the trailer alike. Frost swung his body right, getting his left foot up onto the narrow ledge of the aluminum window frame, then throwing himself up toward the roof. He could see the KGB man now, sprawled back on the far-rear left corner of the trailer—the sudden swaying having thrown him back, Frost guessed.

The one-eyed man was on his knees, pushing himself to his feet, watching as the KGB man raised his silenced automatic. Frost threw himself across the expanse of trailer roof, his right shoulder impacting hard against the luggage rack; his left hand grasped for the KGB man's gun hand, but missed, sliding down instead onto the movielike sausage-shaped silencer at the muzzle of the pistol.

There was a shot—Frost could feel the gun shudder under his hand. Frost, on his knees now, hammered up and forward with his right fist, his knuckles missing the nose, but catching the KGB man's half-turned-away face on the left cheekbone. Frost's already injured hand seemed to scream at him with pain.

The KGB man slipped back and Frost dived onto him, his left hand still on the silencer. Almost mechanically, at the back of his mind, Frost realized the man had to have a second handgun—the shots he'd heard before weren't silenced. His left hand still locked on the silencer, Frost wrenched the gun hand up, then smashed it back, impacting the KGB man's right wrist against the luggage rack. The gun fired again, then sailed into air space. Frost laced his right fist across the KGB man's face, before he felt the cold, numbing pain in his crotch. His breath almost vomited out of him, his body doubled over, the KGB man's fists pounded against his face.

Frost rolled off the man, onto his back. The KGB man was up, his right foot flashing forward. Frost—still winded—rolled away from it but the foot caught him on the side of the head. Frost rolled again, feeling the luggage rack against his back, feeling himself starting to roll over it. Frost caught himself, then threw his weight left, as the KGB man started to kick again. Frost's body rolled into the left foot that supported the man, the KGB man's right foot catching Frost's left shoulder; but Frost's weight knocked the left leg off balance, and the KGB man toppled back. Frost, his groin twisted with pain, pushed himself up onto his hands and knees, and stared back behind the trailer; the driver of the green sedan was reaching out the window with his left hand, a pistol in his fist. Frost's brain commanded his body to move, but another part of his brain told him it wouldn't be fast enough. He half-dropped onto his face, his right hand flashing up under his jeans jacket, snatching at the Pachmayr-gripped butt of the Metalifed High Power. His fingers—almost screaming at him with their pain—clenched around the gun and ripped it from the leather. Frost's body rolled right, a full turn, his right shoulder impacting hard against the luggage rack as he heard the first shot, heard the pinging sound as it struck some kind of metal object. Frost punched the High Power out straight ahead of him, its muzzle canted down, his right thumb jacking back the hammer. The finger of his right hand twitched once, then once again, then twice more. The windshield of the green sedan shattered; the face behind it seemed to shatter, too. Despite the spider-webbing of broken glass, with a roaring sound of its engine, the green car lurched ahead.

Frost skidded on his chest across the roof of the trailer, trying to roll onto his back, seeing the KGB man from the corner of his eye, up on his feet again. He held the silenced automatic in his right fist, his face a mass of blood at the mouth and nose. Frost tried swinging his gun hand on line—his hand froze, so did his stare. Ahead of them was the big eighteen-wheeler moving truck; if it were doing thirty on the steepening grade it was a miracle. And the LTD and the trailer were driving right into it. Frost heard the coughing sound as the KGB man's pistol fired once, then again. Frost started to shout, as the trailer lurched under him.

There was a second pistol in the KGB man's other hand now—a big-bore revolver from the look of it at the muzzle end. Frost swung the High Power on line. The trailer lurched again, and Frost's body skidded across the roofline, as the KGB man fell forward, both his guns going off into the air. To his right now, behind the trailer, Frost could see the green sedan with the dead driver. It was breaking off; the bumpers of the car and trailer apparently had been locked and now were released. The green car rocketed toward the edge of the road, over onto the narrow gravel shoulder, then off into space, disappearing over the edge of the abyss. As Frost turned to fire again, he heard the explosion behind him, saw out of the corner of his right eye the orange and black fireball as the car blew. His right hand moved now, the muzzle of the High Power searching out the target of the KGB man.

And the gunman was there, standing, both pistols leveled as the trailer pulled alongside the massive moving truck.

The KGB man was shouting something. Frost couldn't hear. Frost fired the High Power, pumping the trigger and pumping it again and again. The KGB man took the hits, somehow unmoving. Then the gunman's head snapped back; his body seemed to blow backward off the roof of the trailer. It slapped against the moving van beside them, bounced off it, then disappeared between the trailer and the van. The trailer lurched up, as if running hard over a bump in the road and Frost thought he heard a scream on the wind—"Jesus!" The word fell from his lips, and at the back of his mind the one-eyed man wondered when had been the last time he'd used it with such unconscious sincerity.

He rammed the empty pistol into his trouser band and splayed his body across the top of the trailer—he wasn't moving until Jessica Pace stopped the thing. And then it would be his turn to go to the bathroom.

Chapter Seven

Surprisingly, the store at the campground just north of El Paso, Texas, was still open, despite the hour. Frost paid for the night with cash, looked over the map given him showing the campsite, and picked up a quart of milk and a quart of orange juice; then left. He'd noticed the woman behind the counter staring at him—the dirt, the scrape marks on his hands. Frost had told her there had been an accident up the highway and he'd gotten involved trying to help out. She'd apparently bought the story. Frost glanced at the Rolex on his left wrist—he thought of Bess. She'd be telling him how he'd really gotten into hot water this time—the KGB, the FBI, and the CIA, all out to stop him—and the crazy woman he was shepherding, too. Having forgotten the time, he glanced at the Rolex Sea Dweller again. It was exactly one A.M. He shook his head, forcing open his right eye, rubbing his left hand across his face. "Oh, boy." He groaned, stretching, stiff from the fight and the long ride afterward. He started down the four low steps from the store and headed back toward where he'd parked the car and trailer across the gravel driveway. Jessica Pace had pulled back off the road shortly after the fight and had told something to the driver of the moving van after it had pulled off near them. Frost assumed she'd convinced the driver that she and Frost were feds of some sort—there'd been an almost patriotic gleam in the truck driver's eyes as he'd driven off. Jessica had gone back alone to check the body of the KGB man, Frost having been too weary to walk. She'd told him the body had apparently rolled over the side into the canyon after being struck—that she hadn't found it.

Frost had not believed that, but had been slightly amused at a woman trying to spare his more delicate sensibilities.

When Frost reached the gravel driveway, he heard something, and started automatically to reach for the Browning High Power under his coat. Then he hopped back toward the steps. Three motorcycles raced down along the driveway, big kids driving them—not KGB people or anyone else he should have been wary of, he thought—but the nearest bike nearly ran him down. The guy on the motorcycle shouted something Frost couldn't quite catch and Frost shouted something back—a reference to the biker's affections toward his mother. Frost shook his head, started to laugh. It was obvious the biker hadn't heard him or the young driver would have been back. "Kids," he muttered. He'd held a strong dislike for high-school-age youth ever since his abortive career as an English teacher shortly after he'd been disability-discharged out of the army because of his eye. He tried to remember if he'd ever told Bess the real story behind the loss of his eye. He couldn't remember. There would be no chance ever again, he realized. Jessica Pace seemed asleep in the passenger seat as Frost walked up to the car. He rapped on the glass with his knuckles; the muzzle of her Walther PPK/S .380 rose above the window level before she turned her eyes.

"You do that real good," Frost told her as she cranked down the window and the gun disappeared.

"What was with those bikers—? Almost clipped you."

"You weren't sleeping—just a bunch of rowdy kids though," Frost said, dismissing the subject. "Come on—here's the map. Help me find the campsite—up that way." Frost pointed down the gravel drive into the darkness, then handed the milk and orange juice to the girl through the open window. He walked around the front of the car, standing by the door a minute before getting back in. When he opened it, Jessica looked at him. "I'm a little stiff, that's all," Frost answered to her unasked question.

"Yeah—well, I'll make you a good meal. Pull your shoes off—just take it easy once we get hooked up."

"Yeah—once we get hooked up," Frost groaned.

"Hey, don't bother unhitching the trailer—we're leaving in the morning, no need to. Just do the electrical plug."

"Terrific," Frost agreed. He got the car going and meandered through the darkness down the gravel drive, looking for the numbers. The campground was half-empty and with so many of the campsite hookups unfilled, it was hard to determine which set of numbers belonged to which plot of earth. After missing the spot once and driving around the campground in a circle, they found the spot and Frost angled the trailer in. It was, mercifully he thought, a pull-through. He'd spotted more bikers, including the original three who'd almost run him down, but mentally dismissed their presence. There were a lot of bikers in the world, he thought, and most of them were fine people—or at least as fine as people usually could be expected to be.

They stopped. He and Jessica climbed out, and Frost unplugged the electrical connection between the car and trailer. Having opened the door to the trailer, Jessica set the milk and juice on one of the tables then came out to help him hook up. She began working the electrical connection while Frost fumbled the hose connection into place; he had gotten a pressure valve in Phoenix on Jessica's advice and he first connected this to the trailer intake, then the hose to the valve, then the other end of the hose to the water supply where they turned on the water. They'd used the camper for lunch. Both of them had used the camper bathroom several times, and as he secured the accordian-style sewer pipe under the trailer and then ran out the other end into the sewer outlet, Frost decided that he should open both the gray and brown water tanks. He did this, muttering, "Yuck!" He had soon discovered that the job he liked least in trailer hook-ups was working the sewer connection.

"I've got the electricity—didn't need the dogbone."

Frost stood up, looking at the girl. "The what?"

"The dogbone—it's the adaptor, but they've got the right size outlets."

'Ohh—good," Frost told her.

One more task remained as Jessica disappeared inside the camper to switch the refrigerator over from gas to electrical current and Frost raised the awning over the front window of the trailer—he had to light the hot-water pilot. At least, he thought, it wasn't like Phoenix—windy. It took him three tries with a match—he mentally refused to destroy the wick on his Zippo. But he got the pilot lit, waited a few seconds, and turned the dial for the water temperature to hot. He closed the vented cover and walked over to the door, then up into the trailer.

"I'll have dinner in about twenty minutes," Jessica said without turning around.

"Thanks," Frost grunted, crawling past her, going into the bathroom and turning on the sink to wash his hands—there was no water. "Hit the power switch, huh!"

"Sorry," she sang back. The water gurgled and sounded as though it were about to explode, then started through the pipe.

Frost washed his hands, dried them, and studied

his face in the bathroom vanity mirror. If he felt half as tired as he looked, he decided, he would be dead.

He started out of the bathroom, sliding past Jessica and sitting down at the table by the front window. With only one light on in the trailer overhead, he was still able to see something of the outside when he peered closely through the glass.

"Damn it!"

"What's the matter?" Jessica asked him.

Without looking at her, Frost answered, "Those kids—about a dozen and a half of them out there—split up into two groups, over by the playground area it looks like."

"What are they up to, you think?"

"Well, when I was a kid, I think they called it a rumble. God—that's all I need!"

Frost could feel Jessica behind him. He turned a little, and saw her peering through the window over his shoulder. "What do you want to do?"

"Well—if they get a big, loud fight going, we've got cops all over the place—all over us, too."

"You wanna unhook and get out of here?"

"We do that, we'll have a good stiff drive ahead of us before we find another campground, feel like hell tomorrow morning." Frost looked at his watch again, then added, "It's already tomorrow morning anyway. We can't afford to sit it out too late in a campground—settin' ourselves up for the KGB people, the cops, anybody. We're better moving."

"Want to just sleep in shifts tomorrow?" she asked.

"I'll go outside, see if I can scare them into thinking I'm a cop or something and get 'em to hold the festivities somewhere else—probably the best idea."

Frost started to push up from the bench-type seat, then felt her hands on his shoulders and looked up into her face. "You figure about eighteen of them, and one of you—what if they don't buy your pitch?"

"Well, maybe I knock a few heads together." Frost smiled.

"What if a few of them knock your heads together?"

"I only had one head the last time I looked," Frost told her, standing up, closing his jeans jacket and starting for the door.

"Want me there as backup?"

"No—just have dinner ready when I get back." As soon as Frost stepped out the door, he realized that if he hadn't been so tired he wouldn't have made the decision to brace eighteen or so hot-headed kids all alone—it was dumb. But he was too tired, he realized, to do anything else. Maybe the kids would sense that and pull back, sense he was too tired to fool around, just pick up their chains and switchblades and go home—maybe.

He listened to the crickets and night noises, the gravel crunching under his feet, turned once to look behind him, and saw the warm lights of the trailer behind him. Ahead, under the light of the playground, he could see the dark-clad figures, the voices already audible as laughter, murmuring, a few clear words shouted loudly. The words spelled a fight even if the presence of the two opposing knots of bikers hadn't.

Frost stopped at the edge of the playground, by a rough wooden teeter-totter. The end nearest him was up off the ground and he stood beside it, his left hand resting lazily on it. He said nothing, waiting. After what seemed to him like a long minute, he saw one of the faces turning toward him. The side of that face toward the playground light was illuminated with almost a ghostly whiteness, the other side in deep shadow.

"What you want?"

"Peace and quiet," Frost groaned, lighting a cigarette in the blue-yellow flame of his Zippo—"so go home and grab some sleep, knock off some Zs."

"Go bite my—"

Frost decided, so much for trying to establish rapport with them!

More of the kids were turning around, facing him, starting to walk toward him.

The one who'd talked a moment earlier shouted across the gravel playyard, "What are you, some kind of martial arts expert? You gonna beat us all into the ground, maybe?"

"Just a man who's had a hard day and wants some sleep—you guys rumble and—"

"Rumble? What—you get that outa some friggin' movie?"

Frost finished his sentence. "You guys fight, the cops'll come, there'll be a lot of noise, I'll miss my beauty sleep."

"Ha—looks like you missed it all your life, Gringo!" someone shouted.

Frost smiled, hoping his face was visible in the light. "I take it some of you are Mexican-Americans and some of you aren't?"

"So!" It was still another voice.

"Well, racial and ethnic differences shouldn't become the focal point of hostility—no shit!" Frost dragged heavily on the Camel, his right hand already under his coat, the bruised and aching fingers wrapped tight around the butt of the High Power—cocked and locked.

"Hey, you some kinda clown, some weird social worker or somethin'?"

"I told you," Frost insisted, "I'm a man who needs his rest. Now—you guys gonna get out of here or are you going to cause trouble?"

Finally—Frost breathed a sigh of relief—one of the ones who'd been talking was walking toward him. It was about time, Frost thought. The kid stopped—right in front of Frost and the seesaw. He was about six feet, lean but well-built-looking—the blond hair clued Frost immediately that this was likely not one of the Latinos. "We're gonna cause trouble, mother—"

Frost smashed the near end of the seesaw down hard with his left hand. His right hand ripped the 9-mm from the Alessi shoulder rig; the thumb of his right hand whipped off the safety. The far end of the seesaw shot up, just missing the biker. Frost's left foot lashed out in a savage kick as Frost half-wheeled away, his foot catching the boy in the solar plexus. The loud rush of air was half like a shout, half a curse.

Frost's right fist with the gun in it shot forward, while his left hand grabbed the greasy blond hair, snapping the head back; the muzzle of the Browning

High Power stopped just under the blond boy's nose.

The dozen and a half bikers that had started toward Frost in a rush suddenly stopped—it was the nice thing about a slightly shiny gun, Frost thought. It got attention. "Now," Frost half-shouted, "I'm not saying one more word after this—you guys pile on your bikes and hike outa here—now! Otherwise, blondie gets this right up the old coke snorter, capiche?"

No one spoke; none of the kids in the two rival gangs moved. Then the blond boy Frost held the gun on stammered, "Do what he says—this sucker's crazy!"

Frost laughed, low, near the blond boy's ear so only he could hear it.

"Come on—get out!" The blond boy's voice was cracking. "Please!"

Somehow—perhaps because the word was so little used among them, Frost surmised—the word "please" seemed to have some sort of magical effect. Some of the bikers started drifting back, still trying to save their egos, Frost thought, backing away as if still ready to go into action.

Frost could see the sweep second hand on the Rolex in the playground light as the bikers left, the Rolex was close to Frost's face as it was on the wrist of the hand he had clamped in the boy's greasy blond hair.

The last bike ripped out and into the darkness, only one machine remaining. Frost whispered into the blond boy's right ear. "Now, I know what's troubling you—revenge. Right now, your heart is hardening toward me—I've made you lose face. Well, I can sympathize with those primitive feelings. I really can. But . . ." And Frost paused for a long minute, listening to the fast breathing, smelling the sweat on the boy, the fear there. "If you guys come back tonight, or try following us out of here in the morning, who do you think the first person is that I'm going to kill? One of the other guys, or you? I make my living fighting people, sometimes killing people—I'm good at it. I'll kill you if I ever see your face again. It can be here tonight, it can be on the road tomorrow, it can be in a pizza parlor five years from now. But if I ever see your face you are stone cold dead. No more bike riding, no more girls, no more beer, no more joints—nothin' but dead and six feet under if somebody takes the time to plant you. Now, I want a one-word answer to this—nothin' else. Am I ever going to see you or your friends again?"

The kid sounded as though he were going to throw up when he said it, "No—you ain't—"

Frost pressed the muzzle of the pistol against the kid's nose. "I said one word—no speech. Now—walk over to your bike. I could make you spit on the seat then sit on it; I could make you ride out of here stark naked and backwards. I won't. I'll just kill you if I ever see you again." Frost shoved the boy away from him, leveling the gun out straight toward the boy's face. "Now—ride!"

The blond-haired gang member half-ran, half-stumbled to his motorcycle, jumped it, and started out of the campground. Frost lowered the Browning, stood there a moment until the engine sounds died off, then lowered the hammer on the pistol before shoving it up under his coat into the holster, snapping the trigger-guard shut, then closing his coat. He turned and started walking up the gravel path back toward the yellow light of the trailer.

Afterward, inside, Jessica Pace cleaned his hand, damaged from the fight earlier that day with the KGB man. She rubbed his back for him to relax the muscles in his neck, and told him that she thought he was "O.K.—sort of." Frost took her into his arms, then his hands pressed against the nipples of her breasts. Feeling her hands on him, on his chest, on his crotch, he rolled her over onto her back, slipped between her warm thighs, and told himself some things were better than sleep.

Chapter Eight

Frost snapped off the radio and turned the fan up one notch in speed to make the defrosters work better. It had been almost idiotically cold in the morning when he'd unhooked and they'd gotten ready to leave the campground. And the temperature had been dropping all day.

"Don't get mad at the radio," Jessica told him.

"I gotta get mad at something," Frost countered.

"It's still not cold enough to snow—the guy's gotta be wrong," she reassured him.

"The guy was reading a weather bulletin—an emergency weather bulletin. A freak storm coming down out of the panhandle—dumped twelve inches of wet snow north of here last night. I don't think he was just trying to scare us."

"This is West Texas—it isn't going to snow out here—no—"

Frost glared angrily at the windshield, then flicked on the windshield wipers. "You're right—at least so far. It isn't snowing. It's raining and the temperature is thirty-six degrees. I like freezing rain when I'm driving through the middle of nowhere even better than I like snow. Shut up, huh!"

Frost lit a cigarette, already feeling his steering starting to get mushier—he wondered if it was his imagination. He had never been in a desert during a storm that involved precipitation—and the thought of it scared him. The gas gauge was down a quarter, the map didn't show a town for some God-awful distance yet, and the radio had warned of a blizzard and given traveler's advisories. "Wonderful," he sighed. "Just wonderful. I really like this."

"Are you talking to yourself?"

"I gotta talk to somebody with common sense," he snapped. "Yeah—I'm talking to myself, but now I'm talking to you. Wonderful—snow. God—"

Frost hit the windshield-wiper switch to high speed—the rain, heavy and lemonade-looking, was coming faster now and making it hard to see.

"What are you going to do?" Jessica asked him after a moment.

"Panic!"

Frost said nothing else for a long time and neither did Jessica Pace. Frost watched the rain turn to sleet, then could have almost sworn that he spotted the first snowflake as it fell—seemingly all by it-self—and then was followed by more and more. He cut his speed below thirty miles per hour; his back was aching from constantly leaning down to manually brake the trailer to give himself drag and keep the car from skidding. He turned on the radio again—there was nothing but music. "Can't that guy give a weather report?" Frost snapped.

"Before, you were sore because the announcer told you the weather—now you're sore because he doesn't?"

"Just shut up, will ya?"

"Men," Jessica snorted.

Frost would have looked at her—glared at her he thought—but he didn't want to take his eye off the road. "Snow—all I needed. Why snow?"

"You talkin' to me?"

"No—I was talkin' to the snowflakes. Of course I was talkin' to you. Snow!"

Already, the highway was white and in the surviving west-coast mirror Frost could see the marks left by the car and trailer tires behind him—but there was no other traffic and what he could see of the sky through the swirling snow was dark gray—almost black in spots.

"Snow!"

He lit another cigarette, straightened up against his chair back a moment, then went back to riding the electric trailer-brake lever with his thumb. He thought how wonderful it would be if he crashed into something leaning forward as he was—he'd not only get killed, but break his face first.

Another hour passed—according to the radio—

and now the severe weather bulletins were coming every few minutes, between every song. Fourteen inches of snow were predicted with subfreezing temperatures, hazardous driving conditions, and high winds with blowing and drifting snow. Frost's knuckles were white against the blue steering wheel; his hands shifted the wheel right and left, right and left, searching for traction. The rain that had fallen had frozen under the snow and then started to melt, he presumed, the snow serving to insulate it against the cold. Now, the just-freezing-temperature rain under the snow had converted the highway to polished glass. The wind where it had blown snow off the highway revealed shining patches of slick ice. The car was skidding slightly and Frost worked the trailer brake again, getting the skid under control. There was still no other traffic on the highway and the snow was falling so fast and so heavily that when he looked in the one clear patch on the west-coast mirror, all he could see was a faint outline where his tracks should have been.

"Do you want to pull over?"

"Yeah—I think I'm going to have—" Frost cut the steering wheel hard right, into the direction of the skid, uncertain if, with the trailer, that was the right thing—should he have pulled it left? He worked the trailer brake, but the car wasn't slowing. He could see the shoulder coming up to him, later-ally, the interior of the car. The world around him seemed to have suddenly switched into slow motion. "Get down in front of the seat!" He cut the wheel into the skid and now the car was jackknifing against the trailer. In the rear-view mirror where the defogger had melted away the snow, Frost could see the trailer swinging wildly. He cut the wheel right, then left, then hard left. The car skidded almost backward down the highway. He lost track of the trailer; his elbows locked, his hands braced against the wheel. There was a snow-covered median strip, and the car was skidding backward into it. Where was the trailer? he thought. He searched for the electric brake, couldn't find it as he fought the wheel again. The steering was mushy and useless, the car out of control completely. His fists locked on the wheel anyway, his elbows locked, and his shoulders braced. "Holy God!"

The car stopped, so suddenly Frost forgot to breathe, was uncertain if he could. Then the car shuddered and there was a groaning sound, the groaning of metal against metal, and the car shifted suddenly forward, then stopped—dead.

Frost raised his head, looked at Jessica Pace, then murmured, "You O.K., kid?"

Her hair was in her eyes, her face was white, her eyes wide and glassy. "Yeah—I think—you O.K.?"

"My neck hurts a little," Frost said, trying to turn around, trying to see if there was anything left of the rear end of the car or the trailer.

"What happened?"

"All of a sudden, I just lost it—whew!"

"I thought we were going to—"

"Wouldn't that be insane?" Frost laughed, his hands shaking as he started to light a cigarette then thought better of it—what if they'd ruptured the gas tank? "The KGB and everybody else under the sun out to get us and we croak in an auto accident in a blizzard!"

112

"Yeah—I guess it would," she answered, her voice trembling.

"Stay here—I'm gonna—"

"Not on your life—I'm getting out too!"

"Great—try your door," he told her, suddenly tired, feeling hyperventilated, feeling the adrenaline subsiding in him.

Frost stepped out, his sixty-five-dollar shoes instantly filling with wet snow. He held on to the roofline of the car as he started back, then stopped. The trailer had crashed down on the left rear fender, then bounced away from it. He didn't know if the car was drivable or not. He walked closer to the trailer. The tongue was bent in a sharp right angle and the rear end of the car was half-buried in a rut where the trailer had impacted it into the snow and the sand below it.

"We're stuck, huh?"

Frost looked at Jessica Pace and started to laugh. "I'm sorry I lost my temper with you before." He gestured with his hands. "Before this happened . . . I was—"

"I know," the girl answered.

"And to answer your question—we can't haul the trailer, the rear end of the car is stuck so deep we can't unhitch and try pushing it out. So, yeah—we're stuck all right. And if we don't get into the trailer and get the heat going quick, we're gonna freeze to death. Unless maybe a truck comes along later and hits that same patch of ice, then crashes into us and kills us before we freeze to death—just hope those propane tanks are full."

Frost knew what to do if you were trying to survive a blizzard in a stuck automobile. Run the heat only as necessary, keep the tail pipe clear at all times, keep a downwind window cracked at all times—there was a standard and well-thought-out list. But common sense dictated saying in the trailer—and so did the volume of snow. If the propane tanks went out, he could try to crank the car and use the fuel in the gas tank to heat them. He bent down and unplugged the electrical connection between the car and the trailer. There was always the option of running the car with the trailer battery if need be, or using the car battery for electricity in the trailer. But if they ran out of propane, all the trailer heating system would do is blow cold air, the thermostat constantly calling for heat that wasn't there. He made a mental note to get out several times during the time they were stuck and crank the engine of the LTD to keep the battery alive and the radiator from freezing if the temperature dropped that low.

"We're lucky we're alive," the girl was staying as she started toward the trailer.

Frost clambered over the bent trailer tongue and stood beside her. "You can say all you want," he began, almost affectionately touching the undamaged right rear fender of the '78 Ford, "but there's nothing like a big, full-sized car. If we'd been driving something much smaller that trailer would have pulled us, or maybe turned this car into an accordion."

"I'll get the heat going—and fix us some lunch?"

"Yeah," Frost murmured. He looked up at the sky; he couldn't see it for the falling snow.

Frost shuddered. He wasn't running the radio to conserve the battery; or the heat either, to conserve gasoline. With the wind howling across the snow-covered wastes, the car—the windows frosted over—was like he imagined a tomb would be in the middle of an Alaskan winter. But the engine was responding and running smoothly. Frost kept it running long enough to evaporate any moisture rather than come back the next time and find the engine had seized. His body was shaking, despite the heavy gray turtleneck sweater he wore under the jeans jacket. And his feet were cold. He'd left his sixty-five-dollar shoes to dry out in the trailer and had switched to his combat boots and boot socks—but his feet still felt as though they were freezing. He decided it was psychological. A blizzard in such an ordinarily hot place, in a place where such a bizarre weather situation was even more bizarre.

He turned off the key switch and got out of the car, locking it. He would have almost welcomed a thief. He smiled, his mustache starting to freeze. There had been no one on the highway since the accident—not even a road crew or a police officer.

Frost fought his way back through the drifts, toward the trailer door, clambering over the bent tongue and walking along the trailer body. The snow, drifted around the trailer, was nearly waist-high now. He hammered his fist on the door; when it opened he half-stumbled inside. It was warm, the propane supply holding up—he wondered how long. One light burned in the trailer ceiling; either that bulb would go out or the electricity would go because of the drain on the battery. He could always start the car and let the battery from the car charge the trailer battery, but that would burn up the gasoline. He was saving doing that until he needed to.

"Why don't you shut off the light, Jessica?" he stammered.

"The electricity?"

"Yeah—maybe," Frost said, skinning out of the jacket. He stripped away the last sleeve, wiped off his boots with a towel, and stood up, going over to the thermostat. If they lowered the desired temperature, the thermostat would stop calling for heat and the fan would be used less—less electricity to drain the battery.

"We're doin' O.K., aren't we?" he heard her ask.

He turned around, looking at her. "Yeah—I don't think we'll become anonymous victims of the great blizzard or something if that's what you mean. At least the KGB and everybody are just as stuck as we are now."

"You want some coffee?"

"Only if you give me a whiskey chaser." Frost smiled.

"You got it—hey, tell me about yourself. Like the eye patch—I mean if you don't feel uncomfortable talking about it."

"Not much to tell, really," Frost began, a smile crossing his lips. He walked past her where she stood by the stove, then sat by the table at the front of the trailer, looking through the one bare patch on the window where snow hadn't stuck or drifted, looking at her in the bright reflected light from the snow, the trailer otherwise dark except for a candle she'd lit on the table. "See—I'd always wanted to join the circus, be like my boyhood hero the Great Farquarhdt—he was a lion tamer."

"You're kidding," she said, handing him the coffee and setting a tumbler of Seagram's on the table beside him, then sitting down opposite him, huddling in a sweater.

"No—I'm in deadly earnest," Frost told her. "Well—the circus came to town and I ran off from home, joined the circus—the boyhoood dream only partially fulfilled. After some weeks I got to know the Great Farquarhdt—even let me call him by his right name eventually. Elmo Farquarhdt. Well, he knew I was interested in being a lion tamer just as he was, so in my off hours when I wasn't taking tickets for the bearded-fat-lady snake charmer—"

"They had one woman who was the bearded lady, the fat lady, and the snake charmer?"

"It was a small show on a tight budget," Frost responded. "But anyway, when I had some off moments Elmo Farquarhdt would take me aside. He began to teach me all he knew about lions and lion-taming and about circus biz—it was fascinating. Well, eventually, he started teaching me how to train the lions, to do what he did. There was this one lion—Claude—"

"I always figured they were declawed."

"No—I said Claude."

'Yeah—ohh—the lion had gotten clawed?"

"No—the lion *was* Claude."

"That's just what I said," Jessica insisted.

"Well—the lion was Claude—Claude. You know. Like Farquarhdt was Elmo, the lion was Claude."

"Ohh—the lion was Claude?"

"No—he was never clawed—lions don't claw other lions. He was Claude."

"Ohh."

"Anyway, Claude was the lion Elmo Farquarhdt used to do his most death-defying part of the act with."

"Claude?"

"Right," Frost said. "Elmo Farquarhdt would stick his head inside Claude's mouth—always got a standing ovation. We were in this one town, I remember—Dinky."

"It was a dinky town?"

"No, Dinky wasn't dinky at all—Dinky, Idaho, good-sized place."

"Ohh—"

"Well, I'd been practicing with Claude and Elmo Farquarhdt before we got to Dinky and it was decided I could try Elmo's trick with Claude in Dinky."

"You mean Elmo's trick *in* Claude in Dinky?"

"Right," Frost answered. "But—unbeknownst to me, Claude was having an attack of indigestion—belching a lot. Elmo was used to Claude having indigestion, but never like in Dinky. He didn't want me to go on, but I insisted. Came the time for the highlight of the act. There I was, resplendent in my borrowed knee-length tights—"

"Knee-length tights?" She laughed.

"Elmo Farquarhdt was five feet one."

"Ohh."

"Well—Claude was really troubled, belching a lot. As I started to put my head in Claude's mouth, Elmo Farquarhdt was shouting, "Alto—alto!""

"There was another lion named Aldo?"

"No—Farquarhdt was Spanish, I think. Elmo Farquarhdt was just a stage name. But I did it anyway, stuck my head in Claude's mouth—and then it happened."

"What?"

"This giant belch and his tongue shot up to the roof of his mouth, those huge teeth, my eye going up toward them—" Frost turned away and tugged at his eyepatch.

"You poked your eye out on a lion's tooth?"

"No," Frost smiled. "I pulled my head out of Claude's mouth just in time and rolled across the sawdust-covered floor. Well, Elmo was wearing his old tights and no shoes—and there was a hole in the big toe."

"What?"

"Never cut his toenails, Elmo—walked over to my still-moving body—stubbed his toe right into my—"

"Ohh, shut up." She laughed and reached across the table and hugged him.

They talked late into the night, the girl telling Frost about herself finally. She had been in graduate school when she had suddenly been approached by something she thought at the time was the CIA, but had turned out to be Calvin Plummer's group—an organization far more secretive. She discovered that they had learned more about her than she remembered about herself, that they wanted to have her undergo some specific training, and if she passed it, they would tell her why they were so terribly interested in her. There had been training in the Russian language. She had listened to mysterious piecemeal tapes of a Russian woman, tried to learn to imitate her voice. She had had weapons training, with both Soviet and American firearms . . . martial-arts training, courses in the history of Communism, courses in Soviet daily life. She had undergone a period where she had lived for one year with Americans who only spoke Russian, read only Russian books and newspapers, ate Russian food, wore Russian-made clothes. And then they had told her—about the Russian woman she was supposed to replace. They had surgically broken her leg so she would match the Russian woman physically. They had told her the surgical technique they planned to use on her fingertips and palms was radical, new—perhaps would be unsuccessful. After four operations, she had been shown her fingerprints and those of the Russian woman—she had not been able to tell them apart. She had been told later that by some quirk of fate, the prints had been very close to begin with—perhaps she and the Russian woman were distant relatives, perhaps something else. No one had conjectured why—at least openly. Then there had been the switch and ever since she had been living the life of a loyal KGB agent—waiting for the big intelligence break to come along. The list of double agents in the CIA and FBI was that break; she'd memorized the list, then planned her escape. Once she made it to the President, revealed the names on the list, and was free of what she knew, she would dye her hair, get contact lenses to give her a different eye color, then go off and live in some small town under a new identity. "I have it all planned. They promised before I began that they'd help me when I came back, help me to start over again."

"You think it'll be that simple?" Frost asked, pulling on his coat.

"Where are you going?"

"Start the car once more—then hook up the battery and let the car run and the engine charge us up. The heat's going to kick off. That light I tried wasn't burned out—the power was gone."

"What do you mean, do I think it'll be that easy?"

"Well—do you?"

"No," she said, a curious smile crossing her face like a shadow. "I don't."

Frost shrugged the rest of the way into his jacket and started out through the door.

Heavy trucks were moving in convoy by morning—and the propane had run out as well. The last truck in the convoy stopped. Frost and the girl got their things together and hitched aboard into the next town—to have attempted to tow the car out of a giant snowdrift, in which there was a hole by the driver's side front door, would have been impossible without ripping off the front bumper. The truck driver had given Frost a red bandanna to tie to the antenna of the car as a warning flag that it was there, in front of the trailer. Perhaps that would prevent a snowplow from further destroying it.

The snow had stopped before sunrise, and by noon, when Frost and the girl climbed down from the cab of the eighteen-wheeler, the snow was melting. The street was a sea of slush and muddy water. "Thanks—anytime you need someone's arm broken, call me," Frost told the driver, shaking the man's hand warmly.

"Yeah—thanks, fella. Good luck to you and the lady, huh?"

When the truck had started slowly away from the slushy curb, Frost and Jessica had stepped back to avoid the splash. Frost looked at the girl, telling her, "That guy thought I was kidding about breaking somebody's arm for him—ha!"

She looked at Frost, then laughed. There was a two-story, squarish-looking building at the far end of the street in the middle of a slushy-looking parking lot. A sign hung over the door, proclaiming it a restaurant; and Frost, taking the girl's elbow, started toward it. He was hungry after the drive and for once in his life craved a lot of people around him; there was enough cars in the restaurant lot that it had to be packed.

Frost slung the girl up in his arms and carried her halfway across the parking lot—she wore track shoes and the muddy water was washing over the top of his combat boots.

They had taken little from the the camper—the girl a huge purse with some clothes and her gun in it, Frost a backpack loaded with clothes and weapons. He set her down on the comparatively dry cement apron in front of the restaurant door and shifted his pack into his left hand. "Come on—I'll buy you some lunch, huh?"

"Mister—I'll buy you lunch." She smiled.

Frost shrugged. "I'm not proud." He felt relaxed, that even if the KGB people were moving they wouldn't be moving yet, would still be back behind the ponderously slow-moving trucks traveling in convoy down the highway. Frost spotted two seats at the counter—together—and said, "Over there—come on. I'll order something expensive."

The waitress told Frost where he could find a towing service and while the food was being readied, Frost left the diner and found the garage, leaving them keys to the car and getting a promise it would be towed out within the next forty-eight hours. Deciding this was the best he could do for the moment, Frost started back toward the diner, feeling uncomfortably warm with the jacket over the heavy sweater but unable to ditch the jacket because of the gun he carried in the shoulder holster underneath it. He'd had to pay the tow-truck driver in advance—he wondered if that had been wise as he pushed through the restaurant door. Jessica was still sitting where he'd left her—he'd half-expected her to take off. She was that kind of a girl, he'd thought. She saw him, waved for him to hurry, and he started across toward her. The people in the restaurant had thinned out some and as he sat beside her, he realized they were the only two people at the counter.

"A lot of brave people leaving here," Frost cracked.

"Well—it's melting still, isn't it?"

"Yeah—unless we can rent a car, we'll be stuck here for two days until the car and trailer get towed out. Where's my food?"

"The girl was keeping it hot," she told him, signaling the waitress.

Frost wolfed down the first quarter-pound-sized

cheeseburger and worked on the French fries—it was called a Texas something and he'd ordered two. As the waitress came back and took the first plate and refilled his coffee cup, Frost turned around, hearing someone coming in through the door. Five men—dressed casually with sour faces—walked in. A sour face after the previous night was something Frost could well understand.

"It's Chevasnik and Gorn."

"Is that bad?" Frost cracked.

"KGB—dummy," the girl rasped under her breath. "Five of them."

Frost's right hand was already under his coat, the hamburger in his left hand—he was still hungry and he saw no sense in a shoot-out on an empty stomach.

"Chevasnik and Gorn, huh? I got one of their albums at home—a little on the heavy-metal side, maybe but—"

"This isn't any time for jokes," the girl whispered, her lips sipping at the coffee held between her hands.

"It isn't any time to keep both your hands occupied either," Frost told her flatly. He liked everything about the girl really—except her mouth.

The door opened again; Frost turned on the stool, staring at the face there in the doorway. It brought back memories of Bess. Frost's eye met the eyes at the door; then the face moved out of his line of sight. "You look like you just saw a ghost," Frost heard Jessica Pace whispering.

"No—just somebody who reminded me of one." Frost turned back and faced the counter—the person who'd reminded him of Bess was sitting at the far end of the counter, the five KGB people at a table. The face that had reminded Frost of Bess had been someone they'd both known—FBI Special Agent Michael J. O'Hara.

Chapter Nine

"Who is he?"

Frost looked at Jessica across the French fry in his left hand. 'Michael J. O'Hara—met him on a job awhile back up in Canada. He's with the FBI.''

"Great. We've got five KGB men and a fed—all of 'em out to—"

"Wait up a minute," Frost rasped. "O'Hara's not in on this."

"Then why's he here?"

"I don't know—he's straight, though, like you wouldn't believe straight."

"Bullshit!"

126

Frost glanced down to the end of the counter—the waitress was bringing O'Hara a cup of coffee and O'Hara was looking straight ahead.

"No one moves!"

Frost wheeled in the stool, starting to push Jessica Pace away; five guns aimed at him and the girl, one of the guns a small, Czech Skorpion machine pistol.

Frost kept his right hand under his coat, the Browning half-out of the leather, but not out of the coat.

The girl's hands were near her handbag—he didn't think she'd be able to draw fast enough.

Frost slowly moved his head; the KGB men started toward him. O'Hara wasn't moving—yet.

Frost started to move his right hand, slowly. "No one moves!" the same voice shouted.

Then there was another voice. "FBI—freeze you Commie bastards!"

Snaking the Browning out in his right hand, Frost pushed Jessica down to the slushy floor, then his ears rang from a booming sound—O'Hara's Smith & Wesson Model-29 .44 Magnum. Before Frost could fire, the Skorpion was spraying the counter. Frost, on the floor now, was pulling a table down for a shield; the big .44 was firing again as Frost pumped his first two shots out of the Browning High Power.

There was a coughing sound beside him—it had to be Jessica with the silenced Walther. Frost glanced toward her as he wheeled toward one of the KGB gunmen—he wondered if it was Chevasnik or Gorn. Her purse was still closed, but the front of her sweater was pulled up over her jeans and her blouse was half-pulled-out as well—she'd had it in her waistband, he decided. He pumped the trigger of the High Power twice, then twice more, nailing the man with the Czech Skorpion machine pistol—twice in the chest and once in the head. The pistol fired wildly into the ceiling; fluorescent lights exploded and showered the floor with shards of white glass. Frost pushed the table ahead of him—toward two of the KGB men; the table slammed into one of the gunmen, kicking a Walther P-38 out of his hand. Frost fired point-blank into the second man, two rounds into the neck; the standard blued High Power fell from the gunman's limp finger as he crumbled toward the muddy wet floor. There was a booming sound again and Frost wheeled left—the man who'd dropped the P-38 was on his feet almost as if running backward, the gun in his right hand, a grapefruit-sized hole in his back between the shoulder blades.

There was one man still shooting, his left arm a bloody pulp at his side as he knelt on the floor beside a second man, already dead. O'Hara was bringing the .44 Magnun down out of recoil, swinging the muzzle on line; Frost punched the High Power straight ahead of him, his finger twitching the trigger. The gun in the KGB man's hands—it looked like a Commander-sized Colt—was firing. The man wheeled left, spinning almost like a ballet dancer, then sprawled back across the table behind him, sliding off the table onto his face on the floor.

Frost, the Browning still in his right fist, glanced behind him. Jessica Pace had the silenced PPK/S in both her fists, the slide in battery, but the hammer at full stand. "You got him?"

"Yeah," she grunted, starting to walk forward. She stopped to kick one of the dead men—from the way she did it Frost couldn't determine why she was doing it—to check if the man was actually dead or just because it felt good.

"How ya' doin, Ace?"

"Wonderful, O'Hara—now that you're here, just wonderful." Frost smiled.

"What d'ya say we get out o' here and talk a little, huh—you and the lady?"

Frost looked over his shoulder for Jessica—she had the Walther leveled at O'Hara. As he turned back to look at O'Hara he saw the white face of the waitress—tears were streaming down her cheeks.

O'Hara was staring with his icy eyes at Jessica Pace. "Frost—tell the little lady to put away the peashooter or I'll nail her—and this thing nails 'em good." He moved the muzzle of the 29, but not so much as to get it off line with Jessica.

"Hey—let's talk—good idea," Frost said brightly.

He looked at Jessica. She shrugged, then slipped the Walther back under her sweater.

Frost dropped the hammer on the Browning and stuffed it into his belt. "You got wheels, O'Hara?"

"Have I got wheels? Of course, I've got wheels. It's the United States Government I work for—not some el cheapo government." Then O'Hara turned to the woman behind the counter, smiling broadly at her as he slipped the 29 under his coat, but still held it. "They were all bad guys anyway, ma'am—you know, Commies. Don't cry. Contact your nearest

129

FBI office and you can file a claim for damages—ask for a form—"

"Cut it out, will ya?" Frost almost shouted. "Let's get out of here, O'Hara!"

"Right." O'Hara started for the door, wheeling around once and scanning over the bodies. Jessica was running toward the door, the purse over her shoulder. Frost stood in the middle of the room a moment—bodies were everywhere; broken glass and table settings littered the already muddy floor. He shrugged and snatched up his pack.

The for-official-use-only Interagency Motorpool, gray two-door sedan O'Hara drove definitely had wheels, Frost decided as they stopped on the far side of the small town, but it didn't have a radio, didn't even have a dashboard light—somebody had apparently stolen that.

The ground was dryer here and Frost guessed the snow had not fallen nearly so heavily on the eastern side of the town. "How the heck did you get here?"

"Followin' them—the KGB fellas, Chevasnik and Gorn and the rest of those turkeys."

"Which one," Frost asked, "was Chevasnik?"

"The guy with the P-38—the one I creamed."

"How about Gorn—?"

"Won't you guys cut it out?" Jessica Pace interrupted, leaning over from the back seat and pushing between them.

"Gorn was the one—" O'Hara began.

"The one with the machine pistol," Jessica Pace said, sounding bored.

"Right—you knew them too, huh?" O'Hara

cracked. "Which leads me to why I wanted to talk to you guys—let's get out and chat, huh?"

O'Hara was already sliding out from behind the wheel, the big Model 29 in his right hand. "I got two rounds in here yet—just enough for you guys if I need 'em—now out!"

"I told you," Jessica Pace snapped.

Frost just shook his head, then as he slid out O'Hara rasped, "Hands where I can see 'em, boys and girls."

"You arresting us?"

"That's the general idea—never would have figured you'd be into somethin' like this. Can't understand that deal with Chevasnik and Gorn, though."

"What are you talkin' about?" Frost asked him.

"Assassination—that's what I'm talking about. Now maybe she suckered you with some other story, Frost—make a clean breast of it and—"

Frost looked down at his sweater; it was caked with mud and he could feel it had soaked through to the skin. "I couldn't make a clean breast of anything."

"Very funny—ha-ha! See how you laugh in the Federal University System for the rest of your life, Frost—now let's have the gun!"

"Nope." Frost smiled.

"What do you mean, nope? I could—"

"You won't—at least not until you're sure. Right?'

O'Hara ran the fingers of his left hand through his graying hair, his jaw muscles flexing. "You talkin' truce?"

"Just while we talk—we can take it from there."

O'Hara nodded, then swung open the cylinder on his gun, starting to pick out the empties. Frost's left hand flashed out, catching Jessica Pace's right hand as she started the PPK/S out of her trouser band.

O'Hara's eyes were locked on Jessica Pace, then flickered toward Frost; Frost nodded. O'Hara continued picking the empties out of his gun, then loading single rounds into the emptied charge holes of the cylinder.

Jessica Pace looked at Frost, her eyes cold, the muscles around them tight. "Why the hell didn't you—"

"He's on our side—relax. He's a good guy."

"You'd better believe it, sweetheart," O'Hara muttered, then closed the cylinder on his Metalifed Model 29 and slid the gun into the Lawman leather holster under his coat, covering the gun and the shoulder rig again.

"So—tell me the story, the big picture so to speak—then I'll arrest you."

"I'm gonna load my gun while we talk—O.K.?" Frost smiled.

O'Hara shrugged. "Whatever burns your shorts—loaded or empty, I'm takin' you in, Frost."

"Super—now," and Frost began the story. Knowing no better place, he decided to start with Andy Deacon's urgent request for him, Frost, to fly to the West Coast, ready for work—meaning armed. O'Hara had heard about the fight at the hospital; that had confirmed to O'Hara that Frost had gone bad. Only a bad guy, O'Hara had interjected, would mistreat an FBI agent. Then Frost got to the part about Jessica Pace and the list she'd memorized, the list of highly placed officials in the CIA and FBI who were double agents for the Communists.

"I can't buy that crap—so just hold it right there. I mean, yeah—every once in a while the Reds slip us a bad apple, but we get 'em. There's no big list of baddies who work for the Reds, got the FBI and the CIA after her hide. She ever tell ya the one about her being a Red herself, an assassin sent here to get the commander in chief?"

"The what?" Frost mumbled.

"The President—the President, dummy. You know—used to pay your salary too, years back before you turned mercenary. I guess you guys'll work for anybody if the price is right—never thought you'd go bad—"

Frost pushed himself away from the fender of the FOUO car, his face inches from O'Hara's face. "You dork—why do you think they put out that assassination story? Just to make honest guys like you hunt her down, too! Can't you see it?"

"Hey—I know where my head's at—I wish I could say the same thing about you, Ace." O'Hara grimaced, turned around, walked a few feet away, and stopped.

"O'Hara—she is working for Calvin Plummer, dummy!"

"Calvin Plummer—the superspook?"

Frost breathed a sigh of relief. "Yes—call him on your radio, maybe."

"You can't just call Calvin Plummer on your car radio—where the hell have you been? He's so super-secret he has to open a safe each morning just to find his socks, and I'm supposed to call him on the radio?"

Frost sighed heavily, lighting a cigarette. "Can you go to a gas station and call him on the telephone?"

"Yeah—maybe I can get his number from directory assistance—wait—"

"What?" It was Jessica Pace.

"I got this buddy—maybe. But then what do I do with you two clowns?"

Frost shook his head, inhaling hard on the cigarette. "You leave us here—we can stay over in those trees." Frost pointed to the far end of the roadside clearing. "I can use the shut-eye. Come back, we got it all straightened out—maybe you can help me get Jessica to the President—not to assassinate him, but to recite the list."

O'Hara said nothing—seemingly lost in thought. "How do I know you guys—?"

"Won't go, run out?"

"Yeah—won't run out."

"I'll give you my word," Frost said, not able to keep himself from laughing.

"Yeah—I know. That's just terrific—and then when I let you two escape and you get her to Washington to knock off the President, when someone complains, I can just say you gave me your word and you fibbed—right?"

"Would I lie to you?" Frost asked, laughing.

"Yes—as a matter of fact I'm sure you would. But I guess not this time." O'Hara stuck out his right hand. "Got your hand on it?"

"Yeah—got my hand on it," Frost told the tall Irishman.

"O.K.—I'll be back in a flash—"

As O'Hara started for the car, Frost shouted after him, "Hey—tell 'em I want extra pickles on mine."

O'Hara froze in his tracks, started to turn, then started walking again, climbed into the car, gunned the engine—too fast, Frost thought—and rolled down his window. He looked out at Frost and the girl, then sneered, "I'll get ya extra pickles!"

Chapter Ten

Jessica had wanted to leave as soon as O'Hara's car had gotten out of sight, but Frost instead had taken her by the hand and started toward the trees with her, explaining he trusted O'Hara, that O'Hara was smart despite the crazy talk, and that O'Hara was one of the best men with a gun Frost had seen. All three attributes, with O'Hara on their side, could make getting her to Washington a lot easier—Texas was at best halfway there.

The day was becoming progressively warmer, despite the fact that it was late afternoon by the time O'Hara's car turned off the road and came into the clearing. Jessica had slept—Frost hadn't, not trusting the girl to stay, thinking she might bolt and run assuming O'Hara would be coming back with reinforcements and bent on killing her. As Frost saw O'Hara's car now, he shook the girl by her shoulders; she'd been dreaming—talking in her sleep, half in Russian, half in English. Frost spoke no Russian, but the English words had chilled him. The dream she'd been having apparently had dealt with changing back to her own identity, as if two women—one who spoke Russian and one who spoke English—were fighting inside her. Frost shook her again to awaken her, feeling at least mildly sorry for her and also feeling mildly terrified. He was coming to the conclusion that the girl might be mentally disturbed—there'd been ample reason for it, he realized. But if she were, getting her safely across the country would become even more difficult. As he watched O'Hara climbing out of his car, Frost shook her once again. She was starting to wake up. A chill ran up Frost's spine; his whole body shook with it. What if O'Hara were right, what if Deacon had been suckered, what if the girl were an assassin and Frost was just bringing her to the President's doorstep?

"What—ohh, Frost." She smiled, looking up at him.

"You've been dreaming," the one-eyed man told her, smiling down at her head on his shoulder.

"What's up—?"

"O'Hara's back. He's even smiling. Let's go see him—huh?"

Frost started to his feet, the girl standing up beside him and stretching like a lazy cat. As he snatched up his pack, he felt her hand on his arm. "Frost—let's run. We don't need O'Hara. We don't—"

"It'll be all right," Frost reassured her. "Come on." Holding the girl by her right hand, Frost led her out of the trees and back across the open field. O'Hara spotted them; the lean, lantern-jawed FBI man waved. O'Hara was in his early or middle forties, Frost recalled. He wondered what the man had been like in his twenties—the thought almost scared Frost.

"Comin' O'Hara," Frost shouted across the muddy track; O'Hara nodded back and leaned against the right front fender of the FOUO car.

"Hank—are you sure we can—?"

"Yeah. O'Hara's straight. Listen—it's O.K.," Frost told her again. They were almost within earshot of O'Hara now.

In order to help the girl over a deadfall tree that someone apparently had dragged into the field, Frost shifted his pack a little in his right hand, then climbed the low grade up to where O'Hara was parked. Frost judged the air temperature to be in the mid-fifties at least—the thought of that Arcticlike blizzard the previous night still amazed him. They stopped beside the car, Frost setting the pack on the trunk lid.

"Well, well—glad you waited, Frost—really proud of you."

Frost looked at O'Hara, saying nothing.

"When I was following Chevasnik and Gorn in from Dallas the word was that Jessica Pace was an assassin—right?"

"Yeah." Frost nodded.

"Well—I called Calvin Plummer. Took me some time to get through to him. Found out I don't even have the right security clearance to talk to him. I never liked Plummer much from what I heard about him. Finally got to talk with him, anyway. I like the guy even less now—he's a creep, with a capitol K. But he's one of the biggees, good friend of the President, the whole nine yards."

"So—what'd he say," Frost persisted.

"Well—funny thing. He told me to do something I didn't want to do and I lost my temper—told him to go to hell. You know, in some states using profanity over a telephone system when a female operator might possibly be listening in can get you tossed in the slam."

"Wonderful—what'd he say?" Frost asked again, feeling edgy.

"Well—" Suddenly O'Hara's hands were moving, the little Model 60 Smith O'Hara carried in an ankle holster appearing magically out of the sleeve of his windbreaker. Frost started moving for his gun, but O'Hara snapped, "Don't, Frost—I don't wanna smoke ya, but I will."

Frost eased his hands down to his sides, feeling Jessica Pace more than seeing her as she tensed beside him. "What'd he say, O'Hara?"

"Well—Calvin Plummer gave me a direct order—actually I didn't tell him to go to hell; I told him where he could stick his direct order. Told me to kill you, put the girl on ice some place quiet, and call in for further orders." O'Hara snapped back

139

the hammer on the little stainless-steel Chief's Special, the muzzle of the snubby gun pointing straight out at Frost's head.

"You gonna do it?"

"Not unless I gotta, buddy—no. I'm a cop, not a lousy hit man. Now—do the acrobat number against the car. You've been frisked before, Frost."

"No," Frost said emotionlessly.

"What do you mean, no?"

"What else did Plummer say?"

"Said she was an assassin and that if I apprehended her I'd get a big promotion."

"Is that why you have the gun out?" Frost asked.

"No—what the hell do I need with a promotion? I'm just doin' my job and arresting a pair of suspects. But I'll kill ya if I gotta, Ace!"

"I know you will," Frost said quietly. "I wouldn't expect you to do anything else. I'm telling you that as far as I understand, this woman is working for Plummer. Maybe Plummer gave you some kind of cover story because your security clearance wasn't high enough; maybe he figures I'm more trouble than I'm worth and the operation is better off with me dead. I don't know why he told you what he told you."

"You believe this routine?"

"Yeah," Frost insisted.

"I don't. Personally, I think you're a dupe of the Commies—they don't call 'em old maestros of deceivin' people for nothin'. They got you thinkin' you're doin' this all for Old Glory and Mom's apple pie. Well, listen, I'll go to bat for you at the trial."

"You arrest me, there won't be any trial. Plummer will have me killed, probably have you killed, then get Jessica to Washington to spill her list just like she's supposed to."

"Bullshit—Plummer may be some kind of super-spook, but he can't run around knockin' people off—especially a fed." O'Hara jerked his left thumb back toward his chest.

"You know," Frost smiled, "thanks for reminding me you're a fed." Frost took a fast step toward O'Hara, keeping his hands in the open and not moving for his gun. O'Hara did just what Frost thought he would—backstepped fast, snapped the muzzle of the Chief's Special up into the air and fired a warning shot. Frost dove into him, Frost's right shoulder impacting into O'Hara's gut; the revolver firing again as Frost and O'Hara went down into the mud. Frost's left fist drove up and right, crossing O'Hara's chin; the FBI man's head snapped back, Frost's right hand vised around O'Hara's gun-hand wrist. Frost felt something hammering into his stomach, rolled left, and dragged O'Hara's gun hand with him. Frost's left knee smashed up into O'Hara's right elbow; the gun fell from O'Hara's hand into the mud. Frost rolled over the gun, onto his knees, then up on his feet.

O'Hara was climbing up out of the mud. "You wanna finish this with hands, Ace—or do you and me play quick-draw with the shoulder rigs?"

Frost watched O'Hara rubbing his right elbow. "I break the elbow?"

"Naw—but you made the old college try with it."

"Hands." Frost smiled. Inside him, Frost wasn't about to shoot at O'Hara no matter what happened and he realized O'Hara felt the same—the thing in Canada where they'd fought the terrorists together, been shot up together . . . O'Hara had even saved Frost's life, too.*

"O.K.—hands. Let's do, Frost—"

O'Hara started across the two yards of muddy ground separating them in a dead rush, both arms extended for Frost's throat. Frost sidestepped, his right foot flashing up and out as he wheeled half-left. Too late, Frost realized O'Hara had suckered him, had known that with a high attack Frost would come in with a low counterattack. Frost felt O'Hara's hands on his ankle, felt himself losing his balance and went down hard into the mud, feeling something—O'Hara's foot, Frost guessed—hammering into his left rib cage. Frost rolled left, edging back across the mud, climbing to his feet. O'Hara was grinning ear to ear. "Score one for the good guys, Ace!"

Frost started for O'Hara, planning to sucker O'Hara the way the FBI man had suckered him. Out of the corner of his eye, Frost could see Jessica Pace, the silenced Walther .38 in her right hand, the gun coming on line. Frost sidestepped, shouting to her, "No!" He dove for her gun hand, knocking the pistol off line. The gun fired, its slide as it opened out of battery closing and hitting the palm of Frost's right hand. Frost sucked in his breath hard against the pin; his left fist crossed his body at an awkward angle and punched into the girl's right forearm. The gun fell from her hand to the ground. Frost

*See *They Call Me the Mercenary #5, Canadian Killing Ground.*

wheeled, shoving her back onto her rear end in the mud, then wheeled again toward O'Hara, less than six feet from him, hands spread, his body in a half-crouch, ready to continue the fight. "I owe you one, Frost—but I still gotta do what I gotta do."

Frost sidestepped, snatching up the Walther. O'Hara's eyes froze for a minute on the gun. Frost tossed it through the half-open driver's side window of the car, onto the seat. "O.K.?"

"You're a wonderful person." O'Hara laughed, then came at Frost low. The one-eyed man half-wheeled, sidestepping, and, his back half-turned to O'Hara, his right fist hammered forward to straight-arm O'Hara on the left side of his face.

The tall, lean FBI man crashed down like a tree. Frost dived onto him, his knees impacting against the FBI man's stomach as he rolled away. While O'Hara started picking himself up, he got to his feet and edged back. "That," O'Hara groaned, straightening up, "was a good one—I'll remember it though so don't try it again."

As O'Hara started to move, Frost feigned a low kick. When the FBI man reacted, Frost wheeled 360 degrees and hooked his left fist out toward O'Hara's jaw; Frost's knuckles almost screamed at him as he made the solid connection. The FBI man reeled. Frost stepped inside the sinking guard, his right streaking forward in a short jab to the solar plexus. O'Hara doubled over. Frost's left crossed O'Hara's jaw line; the knuckles were bleeding when Frost caught momentary sight of his hand.

O'Hara was falling back; Frost shot another low, straight jab into his stomach. As O'Hara doubled over, half-dropping to his knees, the knife edge of Frost's left hand flashed downward, catching O'Hara just behind the right ear. Frost stepped back; O'Hara crumpled to the ground.

Frost turned around, O'Hara unconscious on the ground behind him. Frost could see Jessica Pace, the Walther PPK/S in her tiny fists, the muzzle on line with O'Hara's head. "I pulled the chain on him—put the gun away."

Frost stepped between the woman and the unconscious O'Hara. "Hank—I'll shoot you, too!"

Frost, his breathing still labored, his left fist feeling like a toothache, rasped between gasps for air, "You shoot me, unless you get me between the eyes—which would be impossible," and he tugged at his eye patch with his right hand, "I'll get the Browning out and pump you full of it, kid—we don't kill O'Hara!"

"He's with them—you can see that!"

"Could have killed both of us a couple of times, couldn't he? But he didn't. For God's sake, girl—think!" Frost started toward her, fumbling for a cigarette with his aching left hand.

"He'll come after us—then what?" Her voice was shrill, bordering on hysteria, Frost thought.

"I'll fix his guns so he can't use 'em, we'll steal his car—he won't catch us, Jessica. Now put down the gun—now!"

The woman edged back, the muzzle of the silencer unmoving. Frost watched her eyes. "You really got this loyalty trip pretty bad, don't you?" she said, her voice finally sounding under control.

"Yeah—maybe," Frost told her. "Put the gun down!"

Frost watched her moving her right thumb against the slide-mounted safety, then the gun lowered and she slipped it under her muddy sweater in front of her belly.

"You're crazy," she said emotionlessly.

Frost shrugged, turning his back on her, and walked over to O'Hara to check that the man was still breathing. Frost straightened him out on the ground, thumbed back his eyelids. "He should be out for about ten minutes or so—he's gonna be O.K."

"I was worried a lot," Frost heard the Pace woman say from behind him. Frost said nothing to her. He got up, walked back to the car, and got his pack, fishing in it until he found a small screwdriver; then he walked back to O'Hara. Frost snatched up the muddy Model 60, then reached under O'Hara's coat and grabbed the Metalifed and Mag-Na-Ported Model 29 .44 Magnum. He took the guns back to the car and opened the driver's side door.

"What are you doing?" Frost heard the girl ask.

"I'm fixing his guns so he can't use them for a while."

"Why don't you just take 'em and throw 'em in a trash can somewhere?"

Frost looked at her, amazed. "You don't steal a friend's gun—boy!"

"So what are you doing?"

Frost emptied both revolvers and dropped the ammo into his jacket pocket; then with the cylinders still open, he picked up the model 60 and turned the gun over until the right side of the frame was under the screwdriver bit. He found the forwardmost screw, the one under the cylinder cut-out, and started turning it out.

"What are you doing?"

"I'm taking out the crane lock screws on the guns. He won't be able to use them until he finds replacement screws. If he fired them without the crane lock screws in place it'd be dangerous, maybe blow the cylinder out of the frame. All he'll have to do is find a Smith & Wesson warrantee center or a ridiculously well-stocked gunsmith."

"Out here?" and she gestured to the barren countryside around them.

Frost smiled, laughing, saying, "Yeah—out here—ha!"

Frost did the same thing with the Metalifed N-frame .44, then dropped the screwd safely into the breast pocket of his jeans jacket.

He put the partially disassembled guns on the ground beside O'Hara and turned back to Jessica Pace. "Keys in the car?"

She leaned down, looking inside; then her head popped up over the roof line and she nodded, saying, "Yeah."

"Let's roll then!" Frost started toward the car, giving a last look at O'Hara—he was already stirring, starting to awaken. Frost almost envied him—at least the FBI man would be out of the thing for a while. Frost wished he were.

Chapter Eleven

Frost switched on the wiper blades, telling the girl beside him, "We gotta ditch this FOUO pretty quick—this is instant hot sheet."

"What do you have in mind?"

"Steal a car, I guess—since this is all in the name of good old Uncle Sam—I guess once I get you to Washington, the President ought to be able to cool a grand-theft-auto charge."

The girl laughed—it was, if not the first time, one of the few times he'd heard her laugh. "You relaxing a little bit?"

"Yes. I guess you were right—about not killing

your friend O'Hara."

"He's a good guy—he was just doin' his job." Frost hit the wiper blades up to high speed. "I wish this rain would quit."

"It isn't cold enough for it to turn to ice is it?"

"No. When you were asleep," he told her, "I had the radio on. There's a chance of severe thunderstorms, but the temperature should stay in the high fifties, lower sixties—it was a Fort Worth station, so I guess we're driving into warmer temperatures all the time."

"How long before we hit Dallas?" she asked him.

"I guess about three hours—more or less," Frost answered. "I'm gonna have to stop for gas again—maybe I can swap cars when I do." Frost lit a cigarette, watching the rain, slowing his speed a little below fifty. "Why do you think Plummer told O'Hara you were an assassin?"

"I think he didn't trust O'Hara, figured maybe O'Hara was in on things with the double agents on the list. That's why he told him to kill you and put me away, then call him—he would have probably sent his own people to get me and bring me in."

"None of Plummer's people are involved in this, then?"

"No—see, Plummer is technically part of the CIA, but it's a separate agency, completely autonomous. He reports to the National Security Counsel and the President—that's it. As far as I can understand it, some U.S. deep-cover agents have moled into the Soviet Union so well they've been operating for years. With Plummer being independent, changes in political administrations, in the

CIA—none of that interrupts his operations."

"I still don't see why, though, that he helped get out the story that you're an assassin. Isn't that—"

"No," she interrupted. "He's just playing along with the idea—he may be in jeopardy, too. I don't know about that. I think he was doing the only thing he could."

"Still, though," Frost began, then gave up, shaking his head and leaning over to flick on the radio. The rain was slackening, but there was an ominous look to the sky off to his left.

". . . tornado alley for nothing. To repeat, this is a tornado warning for—"

Frost turned up the volume on the radio, listened to a string of town names he didn't recognize and county names—one stuck with him. He'd just seen a sign that they had entered it five miles back. ". . . with softball-sized hail reported—that wasn't a mistake, softball, not golf ball. Hail and damaging winds—"

"Why me?" Frost groaned, looking skyward through the windshield.

"What are you talking about?" Jessica Pace asked him.

"I was just wondering why all this kinky weather has to come down on me—and right now. Why?"

"Well, the climate does seem to be changing, you know."

Frost just looked at her as he listened to the radio announcer recite the litany of what you were supposed to do in the event you sighted a funnel cloud. He left the radio on, heard the weather bulletin repreated, then breathed a sigh of relief when the music came back on. He knew the tornadoes were out there, knew what to do if he sighted one, but being constantly reminded to expect one wasn't something he enjoyed. He started looking for a gas station; it was time to get rid of the car. He glanced down at the ashtray and smiled. It had been full for at least an hour.

There was a large service station just off the road on his right. A clearly marked exit ramp looked as though it led right to it. Frost, glancing behind him in the rear-view and almost shocked not to find a trailer there, started edging over right, his directional on. He eased up on the gas, braking a little to dispel any moisture on the brakes before he actually needed them. He was tired, he realized, having driven through the night after they'd taken the car from O'Hara. Frost was somewhat grateful for the rotten weather—it was keeping the police so busy they hadn't had time to find him with the stolen car. Frost stopped at the *Yield* sign. The rain was still so heavy that he had a hard time seeing through it any great distance and the FOUO car had poor defrosters unless the temperature was turned up all the way. When Frost had tried that he had felt as if he were suffocating.

He made a right, then a quick left into the far driveway of the gas station, pulling up by the far end of the large concrete apron rather than over by the pumps. He turned to the girl. "When I get the car, however I do it, you be ready to run and don't forget my backpack." He scratched his several-day-old beard, then pushed the keys for the FOUO car under the front seat.

"What are you doing that for?"

"Look—once the feds get this back if they can't find the keys, they'll have to get new keys made—and that means they'll raise taxes. What am I—a fool?"

She looked at him a moment, then started to smile, and Frost, reaching across and touching her left thigh with his right hand, said, "Be back in a flash with new wheels, kid—keep the faith!"

Frost opened the door quickly, instinctively pulling up the collar of his jeans jacket against the rain although it almost felt good to him; he had neither bathed nor washed his hair since the last time he'd shaved.

Frost ran his tongue across his teeth as he ran toward the open side door between the two large garage-type doors protecting the mechanic's work area from the rain. He promised himself that as soon as he'd stolen the car, he'd at least find the time and opportunity to brush and floss his teeth.

Frost hit the small door, fought the slick-feeling metal doorknob, and gave it a hard twist, then stepped through, inside. Water streamed down his face from his hair; his eye patch felt sodden, the collar and back of his shirt under the jeans jacket heavy and cold. There was no one in the work area. He glanced to his left and started across the bay past a car in the middle of an oil change. His wet jeans clung to his legs, making him feel heavy as he walked into the office.

He took one step up, then stopped. There was a guy wearing a light-blue shirt with the name "Raphael" on the pocket and around him were two guys dressed like cowboys, almost as wet-looking as Frost felt; and a massive-looking man in a plaid shirt and windbreaker with a truckdriver's wallet in his right rear pocket and a sheath for a big lockblade folding hunter on his hip. All four of the men were staring at Frost. Frost smiled, then looked over their collective shoulders. A small, fuzzy-pictured color television set was mounted on the wall in brackets, the sound too low for him to hear accurately what the news announcer was saying. But there was a picture on the screen—his hair had been combed for once. It was the photo taken of Frost after he'd foiled the airline hijacking some months earlier.* Two men, trying to get the place to Cuba, had used a knife held at the throat of a stewardess as their lever. Frost had stopped them with the help of a woman passenger. A smile crossed his lips a moment as he remembered her, wondering what she was doing now.

The gas-station attendant—Raphael—leaned across to the television set, reached up, and raised the sound. ". . . wanted in connection with a string of bizarre incidents which began several days ago in Los Angeles. To repeat, federal authorities are looking today *for Henry Stimpson Frost,* former captain in the U.S. Special Forces and reputed mercenary soldier. The Los Angeles office of the Federal Bureau of Investigation has warned persons that if Frost or the suspected female assassin he is traveling with should be spotted, both are to be considered armed and dangerous. . . ."

*See *They Call Me the Mercenary #7, Slave of the Warmonger.*

Frost, the smile riveted to his face, walked past the burly truckdriver, reached past Raphael, the gas-station attendant, and the two motorists, and turned off the television set.

He looked at the man named Raphael. "Poor reception anyway."

The truckdriver made the first move and Frost countered the haymaker by wheeling right, stepping inside the truckdriver's punch. As the right flew past him, Frost's left elbow smashed back, into the bull-of-a-man's solar plexus. Frost's right elbow snapped up and back into the chest, his left foot driving down across the right foot of the truckdriver. As the man started doubling forward, Frost wheeled again—this time left—stepping out of the truck-driver's failing guard. Frost's left fist shot out in a straight jab to the man's chin.

The gas-station attendant was already starting to react, a revolver coming up in his right hand from behind the cash register. As Frost finished the left jab to the truckdriver's chin, Frost swung his left out toward Raphael in a wide arc, the fist opening, the edge of Frost's left hand connecting with the left side of Raphael's neck. The gun fell from Raphael's right hand and clattered to the floor.

Now the two cowboy motorists were coming at Frost, their hands reaching for him. Frost's right leg went up, feigning a knee smash to the nearest man. The man started to block it; Frost's right foot kicked out instead. Frost's instep connected hard with the man's left kneecap, his right fist shot up and out, the middle knuckles aimed just below the Adam's apple. Frost's right pulled back, then hammered forward again for a second blow.

The one-eyed man backstepped. The second cowboy, stumbling over the first man going down in front of him started to dive toward Frost who sidestepped. The cowboy bypassing him, hitting into a pyramid-shaped stack of motor-oil cans, that crashed down to the floor. Frost wheeled right, his left foot shooting out and catching the cowboy near the tail bone, kicking him forward and further off balance, into a couch at the far end of the office.

Frost wheeled one-hundred-eighty degrees around to his left. His right hammered forward, clipping the chin of the first cowboy who was already on his feet; the man stumbled back.

Frost started to spin left, then ducked. Raphael, having the biggest storage battery Frost had ever seen in both hands, hurled it. Frost hit the floor; the battery sailed over him. As Frost glanced back, the battery hit the plate-glass office window, the glass shattering.

Suddenly the office was streaming water, the wind outside blowing the rain at them. Frost was half-up to his feet when Raphael came at him. Frost's right punched out into Raphael's stomach; then Frost's left angled high for an uppercut to the tip of the gas-station attendant's chin. Frost was on his feet, the truckdriver coming up from his knees. Frost feigned a right-left, one-two combination; the truckdriver raised his guard. Frost's right foot shot up and out as Frost half-stepped to his left, the toe of Frost's combat boot catching the truckdriver just above the big trophy buckle he wore. The man doubled over and fell forward.

Frost glanced up to the wall rack with automobile keys on it. He snatched an odd-shaped, rubber-backed key. The tag wired to it read, "Tightened belts, adjusted timing." Frost shrugged, glancing into the parking lot. He saw the car belonging to the key—a vintage Volvo P-1800s; about a '67, he judged. Frost jumped through the broken window, over the frame, and into the rain, breaking into a dead run for the off-white two-seater sportster. The door wasn't locked and Frost pulled it open, sliding behind the wheel. "Damn it!" He pushed the seat back—a woman had obviously driven the car there and the mechanic hadn't bothered moving the seat back. Frost found the purse-handle-type hand choke, pulled it out all the way, and turned the key. His foot stomped down on the clutch, his right hand moving the short throw floor-mounted stick into first, his right foot stomping down on the gas as he raised his left off the clutch. The drive-shaft-mounted emergency brake was already off and the car streaked forward, the tires screeching. Frost slowed the car. Balancing it with the gas pedal and clutch rather than keeping his foot on the brake, he stopped beside the FOUO car. Jessica Pace was already out, running around the front of the Volvo. Frost reached across, working the door handle. The woman tossed his pack and her purse through the open door first, onto the jump seat, then almost threw herself inside. "Ready?"

"Yeah—ready," she shouted back. Frost punched down on the gas, his right hand pushing in the choke; the tach raced up over three thousand RPMs before Frost stomped on the clutch, revved the gas pedal, double-clutched to upshift, and did a racing charge from first to third, cutting the wheel hard right as he did. He let up on the clutch; the car stalled a second, then streaked forward. He double-clutched and down-shifted into second, making the turn onto the freeway entrance ramp fast and tight, the Volvo's rear end fishtailing a little on the slick roadway. As it started straightening, he punched the H-pattern manual into third, then hauled it into fourth gear as they jumped the acceleration ramp and hit the highway.

Frost found the small lever on the steering column and flicked it; the red light came on in the dash and the engine noise dropped. "Electric overdrive," he grunted.

Jessica Pace commented drily, "I take it you've driven a sportscar before—I'm glad you can do something."

Frost didn't say a word.

Chapter Twelve

Frost had stopped earlier and cut the covers off an adventure novel he'd been reading to use as backing for the new license plates. Using small wire cutters carried in his pack and practically ruining the M-16 bayonet carried there as well, he had taken the Volvo's plates and cut out the numbers and letters as neatly as possible. Then he rearranged them, using a tube of glue he'd gotten Jessica to pick up at a convenience store to secure them to the book covers, and reassembling the "new" numbers to the exterior diameters of the plates. They didn't look perfect and close inspection would have revealed they were homemade, but from a distance he definitely thought the plates would pass—and with the different numbers, there was a greater chance of evading a casual pickup by a highway patrol car.

Now he opened his eye and looked around him. Rain was still streaming down over the Volvo's windshield.

"Hi—you slept. You needed it, I think."

Frost looked around, saw Jessica Pace's face in the shadow in the front passenger seat. "The rest area, right?" Frost's mouth tasted bad and he didn't really feel like waking up yet. "How long was I asleep?"

"Four hours."

"You get any—"

"No—I figured somebody should sort of keep the watch, stand guard—you know."

Frost stretched as best he could in the bucket seat, yawned, asking half through the yawn, "Did the rain let up at all while I was asleep?" His clothes felt damp and he shivered a little.

"Not a bit—you gonna try driving again or do you want me to do it some more?"

"No—that stretch in the afternoon where you took it for a few hours helped. And I guess the sleep helped too. I'll try the wheel again. You gotta go to the bathroom or anything before I get going?" He started to sit up, stretching again.

"No—I'm fine. No facilities here anyway—we can hit the next gas station, maybe."

"Yeah." Frost grunted. He decided he'd wait too, sat up straight, pulled the choke on the Volvo, and then turned the key; the engine roared to life.

"How come you drove so badly with the trailer? You're doin' fine with this."

"Well," Frost told her, throwing the car into first and releasing the emergency brake, "I like full-sized cars and I like sportscars—not much in between. The trailer threw me. I kind of miss it, though. Maybe I'll buy one sometime."

"What would you do with it, Frost?" she asked, her voice sounding almost sad. "I mean where would you go with it?"

"Ohh—maybe get a Ford Bronco with four-wheel drive, take the trailer up into the mountains, and just unwind for a while."

"You got a girl, Frost?—I mean not just somebody you flop down with—"

"You put things so nicely." Frost smiled, glancing into the water-droplet side-view mirror, then turning on the lights and the windshield wipers. "I had a girl—we were gonna get married."

"For real—I mean, you're not puttin' me on?"

"Why don't we just skip it?" Frost snorted, looking over his right shoulder then starting to pull out of the parking space. The rest area was lit up like something for Christmas, he thought. The trucks parked there had their running lights on, some of them forming elaborate shapes, even faces. He pased several as he started for the rest-area exit.

"If you don't want to tell me, don't tell me—but what happened?"

"I don't want to tell you," Frost said; then, "She died. We were in London, just picked up the ring I'd gotten for her. Old ring I had, got it cut down and a diamond set in it. There was a bombing—terrorists, maybe the IRA, maybe somebody else. The whole side of the first floor where she was was destroyed—didn't even find any identifiable remains. Last I checked they weren't even a hundred percent certain what the remains totaled up to in terms of numbers of dead."

"I'm sorry," the girl said after a long moment, her voice sounding hoarse. "I really am. I bet she, ahh—bet she loved you a lot, huh?"

"Yeah—loved me a lot," Frost said, feeling his throat getting tight as it did every time he thought of her.

"What are you going to do after you get rid of me?"

"Go after the guys that got her—find 'em, kill 'em, keep 'em from killing anybody else the way they killed Bess."

"That was her name?" Jessica Pace asked softly. "Bess?"

"Yeah." Frost grunted as he watched the traffic, its lights blindingly bright through the rain, moving slowly in the opposite direction. "Bess—that was her name. Bess," he said letting the word out slowly like a breath. "Bess." He realized he was gritting his teeth.

"I'm sorry, Hank—I am."

"About her?" Frost asked.

"Yeah—but for a lot of other things, too."

"You think you'll really make it after your thing with the President?"

She was silent for a long time before she answered, her voice sounding almost as though she felt relieved when she said the word, "No."

They drove on, Frost listening to the weather bulletins on the radio, hearing them talking about heavy rainfalls, flash-flood watches, and washed-out roads. He didn't say anything to Jessica Pace, let her sleep instead, heard her muttering—again half the words in Russian. She figured she was going to get killed after she spilled her list, Frost thought. She figured that no place would be good enough to hide from the people she fingered or from the Russians. She was an odd girl, Frost thought. He'd slept with her, but didn't know her. She was changeable—from tough to almost childishly innocent. Her mouth probably made her more enemies than she realized—it wasn't frankness, or thoughtlessness either. It was almost desperation, as though she didn't have the time to phrase something better—had to say it while she could. He'd lived on the edge of things—sometimes thought he was going to die—but never on a daily basis years on end. It was a mental problem and he didn't know the right words to describe it. The troubled sleep, the attitude when she was awake. He half-wondered if, after she recited her list, all the reason for clinging to her sanity would be gone and she'd have a breakdown. And would he be around for it? He hoped not, but wouldn't just run off if he saw it coming on. Frost laughed at himself. The girl needed a friend. "Old friendly Frost," he muttered to the rain-streaming windshield and the lights that half-blinded him. He yawned, settling back and trying to keep awake.

Frost yawned, trying to stretch and at the same time push himself up in the seat; his shoulder and neck ached with stiffness. He stared into the oncoming lanes—somebody really had brights, he thought. The light coming toward him looked like aircraft landing lights. He muttered to himself. "Probably going to be abducted by a UFO now—I was waiting for that to happen. Everything else has."

He tried to look away from the light, but it seemed to be coming across the median strip toward him. "Motorcycle?" he rasped to himself. "Out of control!" he shouted, cutting the wheel hard right to avoid it, reaching out with his right hand, shaking the sleeping Jessica violently, then moving his hand to the stick, down-shifting, cutting the wheel left again, hearing the gravel crunching under his tires. The light was still coming at him—too fast, he realized and he cut the wheel right, down-shifting into first. The tachometer was red-lining, the engine roaring, the Volvo shaking under him.

"Frost!"

"Look out!" the one-eyed man shouted. He saw the trees beyond the shoulder, saw them coming at him; the light seemed to come down at him. What the—"

Frost threw his hands in front of his face and dove down across the drive shaft and over Jessica Pace huddled there in the passenger seat, hearing the crunching of metal, the tearing sound, the shattering of the glass, the roar, then the silence of the engine. There was a hissing sound and he looked up; steam shot up toward the windshield—the windshield was intact. "Get out," Frost shouted to Jessica Pace.

"What?"

"Out of the car!" He reached into the jump seat,

found his pack and her purse. "Come on!"

He looked skyward—the light was bright, over them. And the whirring sound suddenly hit him. "What is it?" Jessica screamed.

"A damned helicopter—run!"

Rolling out on her side after her, his knees in the mud, Frost pushed the woman from the car. The Browning High Power flashed into his right fist, its hammer jacked back under his thumb. "Run!" He shoved the purse at her; she grabbed it and started into the trees. Frost, the pack in his left hand, started after her as the ripping sound of an automatic weapon came at him over the whirring of the rotor blades overhead. Rain lashed down at his face; the spotlight still half-blinded him. There was more automatic-weapons fire. The car behind him exploded as he turned and looked up at the helicopter. The orange fireball blinded him; the impact of the exploding gas tank knocked him to the ground.

He heard Jessica Pace screaming something that sounded dirty. Frost squinted against the light, saw the Walther in her right hand. "Run!" he shouted again. He saw her face in the light from the chopper, shouted at her again, "Run!" Frost, still on the ground, thrust the Browning High Power up, the Metalifed finish gleaming in the bright light. His trigger finger twitched once, then once more. The light was coming closer to him. He could hear the automatic-weapons fire again. He kept pumping the Browning's trigger as fast as he could, the 9-mm bucking in his hands as the 115-grain gilding metal-jacketed hollow points shattered the spotlight and there was suddenly almost total darkness except for the orange glow from the burning automobile. Frost pushed himself to his feet, slipping in the mud, half-stumbling forward as he started to run.

He could see Jessica Pace just ahead of him, see her making it into the trees. Frost hit the tree line and dropped to his knees in the mud, swapping to a fresh magazine for the Browning High Power, then ramming the gun back into the Alessi rig under his left shoulder. He worked the zipper on the backpack, finding the vinyl case by feel, opening it and feeling the butt of the Interdynamics KG-9 in his fist. He fished a loaded magazine from the vinyl case and rammed it up the magazine well of the semiautomatic assault pistol; then he fished into the pack, found his two spare thirty-round magazines, by feel verifying their loaded condition, and rammed the spare sticks into his belt under his jacket—he'd gotten rid of the sweater he'd worn earlier. He closed the pack, opened the bolt on the KG-9, and started to run again; the helicopter was coming back, its running lights visible in the darkness.

"Jessica! Where are you?" Frost shouted.

"Here—Hank!" Frost heard the voice off to his right, still in the trees, and started running toward it, half-stumbling over the girl but keeping his balance.

"What are we going to do?" she shouted beside him over the noise of the chopper.

"Run—fight if we have to—come on!" Frost had the pack on his back now, his left hand free. He grabbed her right hand and started deeper into the trees, the 9-mm assault pistol locked in his right fist.

He could hear the helicopter now, but couldn't see it for the tree cover overhead. He realized, too, that the men in the helicopter couldn't see him either. There was a burst of automatic-weapons fire; a tree limb about twenty yards to their right crashed down. "Come on," he rasped to the girl, starting to run faster, dodging a deadfall tree, almost tripping over a stump from a sapling. He could see a brighter spot ahead, guessing it was the far edge of the tree line. "There—hurry," he told the girl. If they could make it out of the trees while the chopper crew still thought they were below them in the woods, Frost figured, he and the girl might have a chance.

The pouring-down rain was less intense under the canopy of trees, but as they approached the far edge of the wooded area, the tree cover overhead thinned and he could feel the rain more. His hair dripped and felt plastered to his forehead; his clothes were sodden.

Beyond the trees was an open field and past that a road. Frost let go of the girl's hand, checked that the bolt was all the way back on the KG-9, and looked at her. "I want you to run and keep running—if they come on us, I'll hold them off with this."

"That a subgun?"

"No—they invented it while you were away. It's semiautomatic only, but reliable and accurate—it's the best I've got. Right now I wouldn't mind a LAWS rocket for that chopper. Now run!"

Frost half-pushed the girl, letting her get a dozen or so yards out before he started running, making less of a target, he hoped. And if he fired at the helicopter, he'd draw any return fire, giving her the chance to get away.

Frost could see her ahead of him, a darker shadow moving against the night. The rain was coming down so heavily he repeatedly blinked his eye to see. Over the driving of the rain he heard it now, the sounds of the helicopter getting louder behind him.

Almost across the field, he could see the girl, waiting for him by a ditch. He shouted to her, then realized that with the rain and the noise of the rotor blades she couldn't hear him.

His arms out at his sides, the weight of the pack suddenly heavy to him, the KG-9 ready to fire, Frost threw his head back and made a dead run for the ditch. The automatic-weapons fire was already starting. He could see Jessica Pace diving down into the ditch, see a flash from her gun as she returned fire.

Frost was ten yards from the lip of the ditch, when he stopped, wheeled, and threw the KG-9 up on line. Its ventilated front handguard was in his left fist, his right hand vised around the pistol grip. He started pumping the trigger in two-round semi-automatic bursts; the ground in front of him was chewing up as the helicopter crew returned fire. Frost turned, ran, and dove to the ditch. The gunfire louder now. Whoever aboard the chopper was doing the shooting apparently had ammunition to burn, and was firing whatever he had in sustained full auto.

Frost rolled into the ditch, bumped into Jessica Pace's right arm, rasped, "Sorry, kid," then punched the muzzle of the KG-9 over the lip of the ditch and continued firing.

The helicopter began backing off. "They're going!"

"Nuts," Frost shouted to the girl. "They're just establishing a beachhead—landing their guys to come at us from the sides of the clearing."

Frost could see the chopper landing, but at the far side of the field, too far for him to take an accurate shot. He tucked down behind the lip of the ditch and pulled the partially shot-out magazine from the KG-9, replacing it with a fresh one. He had one spare box of fifty rounds in the pack, a little more than enough to load the partially shot-out stick for the KG-9 and the partially shot-out magazine of the Browning. He started doing that, rasping to the girl, "Keep an eye on 'em—" as he sluffed the pack off his shoulders.

He punched the 115-grain JHPs down between the feed lips, loading the KG-9 magazine first. He needed sixteen rounds there. "They're not doin' a thing," the girl told him.

Frost shot a glance over the lip of the ditch as he jammed the last round in place, then whacked the spine of the magazine against the palm of his left hand to seat the cartridges.

He looked back to the Browning, loading it with ten rounds, feeling the magazine full.

"How you doin' on ammo?"

"Got two spares for the Walther, and that's it," the girl told him without looking at him.

"Save 'em—I'll do the shooting. I got more ammo," he said. He looked up over the ditch. He could see the helicopter's running lights, see shadowy figures around it. He sucked in his breath

167

hard, a bull horn sounded from the far edge of the field.

"This is the CIA, Frost—we got you nailed down. Got more guys comin'. Give up!"

"They'll kill me, Frost," the girl rasped.

"I know," Frost told her.

The bull horn sounded again. "We're gettin' you one way or the other—now give it up!"

A smile crossed Frost's lips, his stubbled cheeks creasing with it. "I always wanted to say this," he told her; then shouted, "You dirty coppers—you'll never take me alive, see!" He looked at the girl, saw her looking at him, and shrugged, "I like old movies—what can I say?"

"Crazy," she said emotionlessly; then shouted across the field, "I'm no assassin—and maybe you know that, maybe that's why you want me—"

There was a burst of automatic-weapons fire and Frost dragged the girl down lower behind the lip of the ditch. "Diplomacy struck out, kid," Frost cracked, readying the KG-9, anticipating there would be no more talk, just an assault, the helicopter going airborne to pin them down, a couple of the self-proclaimed CIA men rushing them. He looked behind him, trying to judge if there was any virtue in making it to the road. There was a car parked there—Frost could just see it from his vantage point. "Maybe more of them behind us," Frost rasped to the girl.

"It's a damned hit squad! They're out to murder us," the girl shrieked, taking her silenced pistol, pointing the muzzle up over the lip of the ditch and firing rapid-fire toward the helicopter.

Frost grabbed her arm and pulled her down. "Save the ammo—we'll need it." He looked over the lip of the ditch as he heard the whirring of the helicopter rotor blades increasing in pitch—they were coming. he realized. Frost snatched the High Power out of the Alessi rig—awkwardly—with his left hand, jacked back the hammer, and clenched it in his fist. "I think we're goin' down, kid," he rasped, wanting to follow up the remark with something stirring like, "But we'll take a lot of them with us," but somehow not finding the heart to say it.

There was a loud, unmistakable boom and an almost blinding flash from behind the helicopter. A smile crossed Frost's lips—if Michael J. O'Hara had one consistent ability, it was that he could shout loud. Frost could still make out the words over the noise of the chopper. "FBI—freeze, you turkeys!"

There was a short blast of automatic-weapons fire—Frost saw the flash and heard the noise, then another loud boom and then a scream; then O'Hara's voice. "I said freeze—the next one of you that tries anything doesn't just get knocked on his ass, I'll make chopped liver out of him!"

Frost started up out of the ditch, half-tempted to tell Jessica Pace to wait there, but not bothering since he knew she wouldn't.

Frost started across the field, one gun in each hand, the girl walking slowly beside him. He could hear one of the men by the chopper starting to talk.

"If you're FBI, then get the hell out of here. CIA—you hear that!"

"All I know," O'Hara was shouting, "is that the

next time I shoot, it's for keeps!"

There was another voice, younger, panicked-sounding. "That guy shot my gun right out of my hands."

The first CIA voice shouted, "Shut up!"

Frost, the KG-9 in his right fist and the Browning in his left, stopped a dozen yards from the chopper, hearing the younger voice saying, "They're coming up behind you!"

Frost rasped, "I think I'm with him—drop 'em!"

It was the CIA voice again and from the weird light of the helicopter running lights, Frost could see the outline of the man it belonged to—tall, thin, a hawk-featured man. The rain still poured down. "These people are federal fugitives—we—"

"Shut up," O'Hara shouted. "This gun is aimed right at your head, Florence. If they're federal fugitives, then that's my job, isn't it? CIA has nothin' to do with domestic stuff—or at least that's the way it reads, huh?"

"But—"

"But nothin'. Drop the rods and get away from the whirlybird or your head decorates the side of the chopper—so help me."

Frost kept quiet—it was O'Hara's show and Frost decided the crazy-sounding man was doing all right so far.

"Drop 'em!"

There was a long silence, except for the omni-present whirring of the helicopter rotor blades. Then, the hawk-featured CIA man spoke, his voice low, sounding menacing in the darkness and the rain. "All right—do as he says. But so help me, whoever you are—when I get my hands—"

"Shut up—if you make me tremble in my boots too much I might *accidentally* pull the trigger and blow you away—move it!"

The men—for the first time Frost counted them—five CIA men, or at least they said that—dropped their guns, then started edging back. O'Hara walking slowly out of the trees, the big .44 Magnum in both his fists. "Frost—pick 'em up! Miss Pace—get over to the chopper and help the pilot out safely—get his gun and do something nasty but not too expensive to the control panel so they can't fly the thing. And get the radio, too."

Frost kept low, not crossing O'Hara's line of fire, retrieving the guns. As Frost started gathering up the guns, he felt as though he were in on an illegal-automatic-weapons raid. There was a .45 automatic with a wooden shoulder stock fitted to it; there was an almost unrecognizable semiautomatic sporter, the rifle stock chopped back to pistol grip proportions and the barrel cut to about twelve inches. All the assault rifles were M-16s, selective fire. "Want me to shake 'em?" Frost asked O'Hara.

"Yeah—go shake 'em. May as well have all of it."

Frost started on the nearest man—the hawk-featured one—and as he searched each man in turn he added to the pile of guns, trying to keep mental tally. Three snubby .38s—one guy had carried two of them—and five 9-mm autoloaders, four lock-blade folding hunters—he finally gave up.

Frost started emptying the guns, then stripped them, snatching parts here and there and throwing the ammo into the darkness. He kept the three revolvers, since he didn't feel like fishing in his pack to get a screwdriver for them.

Frost looked up to see Jessica Pace stepping out of the helicopter. "They're going to need a whole new interior." She laughed. Frost liked it when she did that.

"Nothin' too expensive—I told you that." O'Hara groaned. "I might have to pay for it."

The hawk-faced CIA man shouted, "You'll have to pay for this, all right."

"Yeah? Well—go suck an egg," O'Hara snapped back. "Let's get out of here, Frost," O'Hara shouted. Frost, both guns trained again on the CIA men, started to back away.

His eye riveted on Jessica Pace— she was holding a revolver, apparently the one taken from the helicopter pilot. She had it pointed, her arm straight out in front of her, at the hawk-faced CIA man. Frost shouted at her, "No, Jessica—don't!"

O'Hara was shouting, "Pace—pull that trigger and so help me, I'll drop you where you stand, woman!"

"Why?!" She screamed in the darkness, the rain drumming harder now. "Why? They would have killed us, all of us. That's what they were here for. A damned hit team, that's all they are. They don't see; they don't want to see! No—"

"Jessica!"

The girl turned, looking at him by the glow of the running lights as Frost shouted at her. "If we let 'em go, Jessica, they'll, ahh—" Frost was trying to come up with a reason.

"If you shoot, and I shoot you, lady," O'Hara shouted from behind Frost, "then all of it's for nothing. You'll never get where you want to go. They'll have won and you'll have given it to 'em on a silver platter."

Frost watched what he could see of her face and O'Hara's words had apparently clicked with her. She lowered the gun to her side, letting it hang limply as she started walking toward Frost, then past him. Frost stopped her, almost gently taking the gun from her hand. Side by side, Frost and O'Hara backed out of the clearing.

Once, Frost caught a look at O'Hara's face. It registered what Frost was feeling in his guts, registered something he hadn't wanted to say but realized both he and O'Hara knew.

Jessica Pace was cracking up, going progressively more homicidal, more irrational. And the thought that he had her only marginally more than halfway to Washington scared Frost to death.

Chapter Thirteen

Frost had debated what was the more pressing need. He'd decided to brush his teeth first—then shave and shower. He brushed twice, almost rubbed the dental floss through the skin of his gums, then shaved, the Norelco balking only slightly at the multiple days' beard growth. Now, after washing his hair and his body at least twice, the one-eyed man stood under the hot steaming water and tried to relax.

He'd let Jessica shower first and she'd promptly fallen asleep on the bed in the motel room. O'Hara had the adjoining room and was now sitting in their room, watching a western on one of the television movie channels cabled into the set. Frost let out a long sigh. He wondered where it would end.

After leaving the CIA people with the disabled chopper, they'd tossed the revolvers and spare parts Frost had lifted from the other guns into the trunk of O'Hara's FOUO car. It was the same car—O'Hara had gotten it back. As they'd driven away, O'Hara had seemingly felt immediately compelled to tell them how he'd followed them—and rescued them. After the fight with Frost, O'Hara has awakened, fumed over what Frost had done to his guns, then hitchhiked back into the town where there had been the fight with the KGB people under Chevasnik and Gorn. There was a U.S. Border Patrol Station there and using his FBI identification, along with the help of the border patrol, he'd gotten the tow-truck operator to get him out to Frost's trailer and car. O'Hara had searched both. He'd gotten the car freed up and found it in perfect running condition except for the smashed-in left rear fender. O'Hara had taken what personal articles he could find that belonged to Frost and the girl, then he'd taken their car. The armorer at the border patrol station had been friends with a local gunsmith who had supplied the crane lock screw for O'Hara's N-frame model 29 and the armorer himself had been able to come up with the J-frame screw for O'Hara's little .38 special Model 60. Using Frost's car, and his guns working again, O'Hara had set out after Frost and Jessica.

Assuming Frost had no choice but to head for the Fort Worth/Dallas area, O'Hara—with the help of a borrowed magnetic Mars light and the use of his Federal I.D. for the few persistent highway-patrol people who'd stopped him—had pushed one hundred miles per hour whenever weather had allowed. He'd reached the service station where Frost had ditched the FOUO car and stolen the Volvo about six hours after Frost had gone. Telling the local police Frost had been assisting a federal investigation, he'd gotten the heat backed off slightly on the auto theft charge and gotten his own FOUO car out of the police impound lot, then continued on. With the radio in the FOUO car, he'd picked up the air-to-ground transmissions between the helicopter and their back-up units on the ground; that led him—he'd admitted with a generous amount of luck—to where Frost and the girl had been cornered by the CIA helicopter crew and its hawk-faced leader.

As Frost toweled down, then pulled on fresh clothes, he decided O'Hara had seemed relatively pleased with himself. Frost studied his face in the mirror again as he put on a fresh black eye patch, crumpling the paper cover and throwing it away. It was fast getting to the point where he would no longer be able to avoid getting into a shoot-out with federal authorities—and despite the girl's story, Frost was in no way eager to start shooting at men who were on the same side he was. If the girl's story was wholly true, at the worst, the men who were leading the field operations could be Communist doubles—which meant the men Frost would wind up trading shots with would be nothing more than patriotic guys doing their duty—they supposed.

He shook his head, noted the added gray hairs in his sideburns, and walked through the bathroom doorway, flicking off the light. O'Hara was just watching the end of the western. Frost poured himself a drink from the quart bottle of Meyers rum. He smelled the dark liquid in the motel-room glass, then sipped at it, its warmth assailing his throat and stomach almost instantly.

"You've got good taste in liquor, O'Hara," Frost remarked.

The icy-eyed FBI man looked up from the television set, smiled, and nodded.

"Got lousy taste in friends, though."

"Yeah, well . . ." Frost laughed.

O'Hara stood up and flicked off the television, glancing back over his shoulder at Jessica Pace as was Frost. Frost had never seen her sleep so peacefully. "What—you mickey her?" Frost asked.

"Naw—never do that with girls—just gave her two healthy shots of the rum there and as tired as she was, she conked out."

"Good." Frost nodded, sipping again at the dark rum.

"You hold onto my crane lock screws? It irks me to have blue screws on a stainless gun and a Metalifed one."

"Yeah." Frost nodded, finding his jeans jacket, then fishing in the breast pocket. He handed them across to O'Hara; the FBI man already held a small screwdriver in his hand.

"Good—at least I'll give you that. Ya didn't throw 'em away."

O'Hara sat down at the table by the motel-room

window, pulled the Model 29 out of the Lawman leather rig on the dresser, unloaded it, and started to turn out the incongruous-looking blue screws.

Frost poured himself more of the rum, then sat down opposite O'Hara. Frost had cleaned his guns earlier while Jessica had taken a shower. Without looking up from his work, O'Hara asked, "You think the dame is bonkers,e right"

Frost's eye hardened as he looked past O'Hara to the girl sleeping on the bed.

O'Hara looked up. "If she didn't wake up when the Indians attacked Fort Apache, she won't wake up now. Answer my question." O'Hara set the Model 29 aside, reached down under the table, and pulled the little Model 60 from the ankle holster, unloading it and then backing out the blued screw.

"Maybe." Frost sighed. "Maybe she is—but if she is, it's more like battle fatigue."

"I see ya been thinkin' about it, though, huh?"

"Yeah, well—"

"Look, Ace—if she is, we may have mucho problems. Ya know?"

"What made you bail us out back there?" Frost asked.

"About time you asked me that—beginnin' to think you took me for granted or somethin'. It was all because you didn't shoot me—or let her shoot me." O'Hara jerked his thumb over his shoulder toward the sleeping Jessica. "I was watchin' the superspook there with that wheel-gun she took off the chopper pilot. She was gonna ice everybode right there—not battin' an eye, either."

"She's been in a rough game the last few

yeara—and she didn't choose it either. Plummer just recruited her because she looked like the Russian girl she substituted for. Pulled her out of grad school, gave her the spy-school routine, and then told her about the job, almost brainwashed her into it."

"Yeah, well—looks like she got the hang of it all right."

"Just what are your plans—now that you rescued us from the jaws of death and that whole bit?" Frost laughed, trying to change the subject and lighting a Camel in the blue-yellow flame of his battered Zippo.

"Help get ya to Washington—but not to the President."

Frost sat bolt upright.

"Relax—I got a compromise you'll love. Makes good sense too. Get her to Plummer. If Plummer didn't trust me on the phone and doesn't trust you, gettin' his prize agent back to him oughta show him we're on the up and up. Right?"

Frost nodded, sipping at more of the rum.

"So, fine—Plummer takes her to the President, or tells us to do it, but we get to check her out first before springin' her on the old chief executive. There's still that assassin story. But I get more and more to where I don't buy that—nobody in his right mind would pick a dame like that for an assassin. Blows her cool too much, too eager to knock off folks—know what I mean?"

"Yeah." Frost groaned. "I know what you mean."

"Take you, for example—you'd be a lousy assassin." O'Hara laughed. "Lose your temper too much. Your only good quality is persistence—you're stubborn."

"I wish I could give you a compliment." Frost laughed. "But I hate to lie."

"Bite it," O'Hara cracked, starting to reload his 29 and the little Model 60. "Oughta get yourself a revolver, Frost—cut out all this automatic-pistol nonsense. Get yourself one of them new stainless .44 Magnum 629s—now that's a honey of a gun. That little pipsqueak 9mm you like won't knock a guy down unless you fill him full of holes."

"No—you miss the idea," Frost told O'Hara, keeping his face straight. "This one time I was in a windstorm, fightin' some bad guys holed up behind a wrecked automobile. Workin' with a cop who carried a .44 just like you do. Well—two of the guys we were after started out from behind the car, firing subguns, the whole bit. My buddy with the .44 shot the one guy and I shot the other guy with my 9mm. A big, superstrong gust of wind came along—right? Blew over the guy I'd shot. But the one my buddy had plugged with the .44—the wind blew right through the hole and the guy just kept shootin'. Let me tell ya'—"

"Aww, shut up, Frost. You and them sick jokes!"

"You didn't spring your master plan on Jessica Pace yet, did you—about the Plummer detour before she sees the President?"

O'Hara stood up, smiling. He slipped the Lawman leather shoulder harness across his back, anchored the .44 to his belt to keep the holster from swinging out, then bent down to put the little .38

180

back in his ankle holster.

"Well?" Frost persisted.

"Naw—figured I'd let you do that, sport—since you know the lady better, she trusts you more. She still doesn't trust me. Just watch out she doesn't give me an ice pick in the kidney or somethin' when I'm eatin' a pizza." Then the smile faded from O'Hara's face. "I'm not kiddin'—I think she still figures I'm up to somethin', settin' her up. And she'd kill me as soon as look at me. And maybe you, too, Frost. Take this the way I intend it, huh? But I'm glad it's you sleepin' with her and not me. I'd be scared to death to close my eyes."

"I don't have that problem—eyes," Frost said, trying to laugh and realizing he couldn't.

O'Hara started for the door. "I got a wake-up call in for both rooms at seven—see ya in the mornin'." O'Hara's hand was already on the doorknob, the sportcoat draped over his left shoulder, covering his gun. "Hey—incidentally. How's Bess—now there's a hell of a nice dame—"

"She's dead, Mike," Frost told him, realizing O'Hara probably wouldn't have known. Frost suddenly wondered why he'd called the man by his first name.

"She's what—? She was doin' fine when I left Canada—at the worst she would have been in a wheelchair; but dead?"

"It wasn't that," Frost said, his voice low, his throat tight-feeling. "She recovered from the bullet wounds, had the operations for her hip, was perfectly fine. Had this little scar from the operation on her—" and Frost suddenly felt embarrassed talking about it, revealing an intimacy. "No. We were—"

"How'd it happen?" O'Hara demanded, turning around, staring at Frost.

"We were in this store in London, were going back stateside to get married. Some goddamned terrorists put a bomb in the store and—" Frost downed the rest of his drink.

O'Hara sat down on the luggage stand by the door. "God, man—I didn't—I'm sorry, Hank. I mean really sorry. She was so—"

Frost inhaled hard, lighting another cigarette, almost choking on the smoke because his throat wasn't working right. "Yeah—she was so—"

Chapter Fourteen

"There's a roadblock up there—I don't think we're easin' through this one, guys," O'Hara rasped through his gritting teeth.

Frost looked across the wheel of the rented Ford Granada, then glanced back to O'Hara, peering over the front seatback between Frost and the girl. "What now, FBI person?" Frost asked.

"What you mean we, paleface?" O'Hara laughed. "Let's turn off—try to make it look inconspicuous. Could be a driver's license check, you know."

"My rear end," Frost answered.

"Yeah—well, that too. Naw. You're probably right—the Mississippi cops are lookin' for us. Couldn't be lookin' for the car, though—unless the guy at the rental agency made me. Can't see 'em puttin' out an APB on a fellow fed though," O'Hara groused.

Frost spotted a side road of the highway—they'd avoided the Interstate—and took it. O'Hara had rented the car early in the morning, leaving the FOUO car in the parking lot of a twenty-four-hour supermarket; then they'd started heading out of Louisiana for the Mississippi line. They'd passed state troopers twice and there hadn't been as much as a flicker of a Mars light, Frost thought. But the roadblock at the border into Mississippi had to be for them.

Frost went slowly down the side road—it was in clear view of the roadblock still.

"You finked on us, O'Hara—at that last gas station," Jessica Pace shouted suddenly.

"What? You're bananas, lady—why the heck would I rat on you when I'm workin' with you?"

"It's a trap, just a con to get us off guard. That whole CIA thing last night, then you showin' up. Just to sucker us into a better spot for them to nail us without too many of them getting it. Or maybe they want to get me alive so they can get me to tell them something—that's how the Commies work, they—"

"Now shut up!" Frost realized he was losing it, losing control, losing his temper. "Just shut up. O'Hara is my friend, he's trying to be your friend. You don't know what you're saying."

"A Commie'd sell out his own mother!" Jessica Pace shrieked.

"Well . . . I can't argue with that," O'Hara said with what Frost labeled almost insane calm. "But I ain't a Commie, girl—see!"

"O'Hara—Jessica—just both of you—or so help me," Frost realized he was shouting; what he was saying was incoherent, didn't make any sense. "Damn it!"

"He's gonna put us away, Hank!"

Frost started to say something back to the girl, but O'Hara, his voice odd-sounding, cut him off. "No, lady—I'm not, but maybe they are!"

Frost glanced into the rear-view mirror, just catching sight of an airplane disappearing over the car.

"Get over there," O'Hara rasped, leaning forward into the front seat, apparently trying to look up through the top of the windshield. "Look at that! A lousy airplane—they got us spotted."

"Cops or the feds?" Frost grunted.

"Naw—KGB. I'll lay ya money on it. Looks like the shootin' war's got itself started, guys," O'Hara snarled. The FBI man leaned back from the front seat, Frost moving the mirror down to watch him. O'Hara had the big Metalifed Smith & Wesson .44 Magnum out of the shoulder rig under his coat, the cylinder swinging out, then closing in his hands. "Never shot down an airplane with one of these—but if they start shootin' at us, they can kiss that single engine good-by."

There was a faint whistling sound, then suddenly the front end of the car was shuddering, the steering not responding under Frost's hands; there was a burst of light, dirt and gravel rained down on the hood of the car.

"For God's sake, Frost—you don't drive worth a—"

"Shut up, O'Hara," Frost rasped through his teeth, his lips bared, his knuckles white on the steering wheel as he fought the car back onto the road, the plane off to his far right. "That was a bomb—maybe a grenade. I've had it—really had it with accidents, with cars, with driving this woman from one end of the country to the other!"

"Those weren't Mississippi cops at that roadblock," O'Hara muttered.

"I've had it with automobile accidents, with people I don't even know shooting at me! What the hell is—"

The plane was coming back and Frost shut up. He felt foolish, angry and disgusted. As the plane made another low pass he saw a small dark object drop out of it and he felt semiterrified. "Grenade!" Frost shouted, cutting the wheel hard left to avoid it. The concussion rocked the car. Frost cut the wheel left again as the dirt and gravel streamed down on the hood of the car and across the windshield.

"Look out for that tree!" It was the girl shouting.

Frost tried pulling the steering wheel hard right, but the steering wasn't working. The hood had popped up in front of him. Frost tried the brakes and when they didn't stop him fast enough he tried the transmission; he realized the grenade had knocked out the engine. "Get down—we're gonna—"

Frost's hands and wrists and forearms and then his shoulders, shuddered. His forehead hammered forward into his right fist still locked on the steering wheel, his head bouncing back as he rolled down toward Jessica Pace. The car stopped dead and Frost rolled to the floor.

He opened his eye, not knowing if he'd been unconscious or not; his head ached.

Jessica Pace was beside him, on the floor of the front seat. Frost heard O'Hara. "Out of the car—quick! They're comin' after us!"

Jessica Pace was already moving, the little Walther PPK .38 with the funny-looking silencer at its muzzle clenched in her tiny, right fist. Frost pulled himself across the seat, like a swimmer, his hands ahead of him, clawing at the fabric. He half-rolled, half-fell to the ground. O'Hara shoved his pack at him and Frost started to his feet. His ears ached suddenly as the big .44 Magnum went off too close to him. "Put a muffler on that thing!" Frost snapped, on his feet, slinging the pack across his back, the KG-9 in his right hand, the two spare magazines rammed into his trouser belt.

"Lay down some fire on that plane, Frost, and stop complainin'," O'Hara shouted.

"Bite it," Frost retorted, then grasped the ventilated barrel shroud of the KG-9 in his left fist, the thirty-two-round magazine already loaded up the well, the bolt already back. Frost's right fist tightened around the pistos grip, the first finger of his right hand pumping the trigger. He started running, the KG-9 spitting two-round bursts as he moved.

The plane was making another low pass and cars

from the "police" barricade were streaming up the side road toward the wrecked Ford Frost had piled into the tree. His head still aching, Frost shouted, "Grenade!" The small single-engine plane made another low pass along the ground. Frost hit the ground, rolling, covering his face with his hands. He heard the booming of O'Hara's .44 Magnum, then looked up. The windshield of the lead car was shot through; the car piling off the road, roaring into a ditch. Frost rolled to his knees, the KG-9 in his fists, its trigger pumping as the small aircraft started to climb, away from him, into the low clouds over a stand of pines. The KG-9 bucked slightly in his hands as Frost kept elevating the muzzle, the aircraft almost out of range. Mentally keeping count, he guessed at four rounds left in the magazine—Frost pumped them out as fast as he could pull the trigger.

The single-engine plane seemed to stall in midair; then Frost dove for the ground. The forward portion of the fuselage exploded, leaving Frost's ears ringing with the sound. He looked up, his right eye squinted against the black, oily smoke and the debris. More explosions, smaller than the first, belched from the tumbling aircraft—the grenades, he thought. There was a whistling sound, almost like an air-raid siren. It grew louder and more intense as the aircraft, belly-flopped, then half-glided back into the stand of pines. There was another explosion, then an orange-and-black fireball gushed upward out of the trees.

Frost was on his feet, ramming the next magazine into the KG-9. O'Hara shouted behind him, "Nice one, Ace—come on!"

Frost wheeled, pumping a half-dozen rounds from the KG-9 at the five cars speeding toward him along the side road fifty yards to his rear. Then he bent low, wheeling, starting into a dead run.

Frost could see Jessica Pace, ahead of him, stopping every few yards, spinning around, firing two-round bursts from the little Walther .38. O'Hara was on one knee, the gleaming .44 Magnum in both fists, the six-inch tube jerking upward as the booming of the big-caliber handgun reached Frost's ears. Frost spun around, dropping low, firing at the men streaming from the cars along the road. The faces were Slavic-looking, their guns a collection of automatic weapons not common in domestic police arsenals. O'Hara had been right, Frost thought. It was the KGB. Frost could hear the Model 29 booming again, see one of the KGB men flying backward, his assault rifle falling from his hands, the hands going up to the chest.

"Ha! Ha!" It was O'Hara. "Got one!"

Frost pumped the trigger on the KG-9, ripping a ragged, vertical line of red into the neck and face of a mustached man holding an AK-47. The man spun around crazily, then collapsed into a heap on the ground, and AK-47 firing into the muddy dirt at his feet as he fell.

Frost got to his feet again, hearing the 29 boom once more, and catching a glimpse of O'Hara cramming a speed loader against the cylinder of the N-frame Smith, then starting to run. Jessica Pace was about twenty yards ahead of him, Frost judged, on one knee, firing the little Walther. Frost shot a glance behind him. One of the KGB men snapped his head back, dropped his gun; his face was a mass of red, his body was collapsing forward.

Frost, without looking, snapped off two two-round bursts behind him. There was a drainage ditch of some kind up ahead and he aimed for it. Already the volume of fire from the dozen and a half KGB men was heavy and once they organized into more than a group of running, shooting, and hollering gunmen, the fire would get heavier.

"The ditch—over there!" Frost shouted, seeing O'Hara, then catching sight of the FBI man nodding. "Jessica—make for the ditch," Frost shouted. The girl didn't seem to register anything on her face—that she'd heard Frost or even cared—but she changed the direction in which she ran, still pumping the Walther again, the absence of noise when the gun discharged almost making it seem unreal, as if she were a child playing cops and robbers or cowboys, and not firing real bullets at men firing back.

Frost emptied the KG-9's magazine and bent low, running, trying to swap magazines as he moved. The ground around his feet was ripping up and Frost could hear whining sounds, like those made by huge insects; the sounds whistled past his ears, surrounding him. He remembered a tour of guard duty back in his early days in the military, the flies, so thick in the night air that he could feel them around his face, parting like a wave as he'd walked. He could hear the buzzing sounds near his ears, waited for the sensation on his skin that one of them was sucking his blood. He felt an impact now, on the left side of his neck, started falling forward, but kept his gun up out of the mud as his face slammed into it, his mouth tasted it. Frost ran his left hand up to his neck and it came back wet, sticky.

He rolled onto his back, snatching the KG-9 up on line and pumping the trigger twice; two of the KGB men coming at him in a rush from ten yards behind, went down.

Frost pushed himself to his feet, fired another two-round burst, caught another KGB man—blond, long-haired and thin-faced; the man grabbed at his crotch, doubling over. Frost thought he heard a curse coming from the man's lips over the roar and whine of gunfire.

When Frost started to run again, he heard the almost-reassuring sound of O'Hara's Model 29, and shooting a glance over his right shoulder he saw one of the KGB-ers go down.

The ditch was less than a dozen yards ahead. Frost ran for it, the KG-9 in his right hand. He could feel the wetness of his neck wound as the blood dribbled down into his shirt—the burning, almost-itching feeling. The lip of the ditch was a yard away now, the volume of fire around him suddenly increasing. As Frost dove for it he heard O'Hara's N-frame Smith booming again, its noise almost deafening him. Frost hit the ditch and rolled down, wetting the left side of his face with the brackish water as he did so. Then he pushed himself up to his knees, and poked the muzzle of the KG-9 over the lip of the ditch.

O'Hara was muttering something. Frost looked to his left, toward the man's face.

O'Hara's icy eyes locked on Frost; the FBI man

said, "You know—I lost six rounds of once-fired empties back there when I reloaded—boy! Those suckers are gonna pay for that!" And the big .44 Magnum revolver boomed again. Frost looked to his right. A KGB man went down, rolling across the mud, his AK-47 discharging a fast burst into the air.

Shaking his head, almost smiling, Frost started pumping the trigger of the KG-9 9mm, nailing one, then a second, then a third KGB man. He fired at a fourth man, clipping the man in the shoulder; two of his comrades grabbed at him, dragging him off, his heels in the mud, one of the men still firing. Frost started to fire at the man, then let it go; he'd never shot a man hauling a wounded buddy to safety and he wasn't about to start. The thought amused the one-eyed man for a moment—did KGB men really have buddies? Maybe wives and children? Was he getting soft? he wondered. Frost fired the KG-9, nailing a hulkingly tall man with a submachine gun, running dead on for the ditch. Frost's first round slammed against the man's chest—Frost could see him lurch back, then keep on running. Frost's second round hit the throat. The big man's left hand started to grasp for the wound; then the man spun out and collapsed into the mud.

The KG-9 was empty.

Frost snatched the Metalifed Browning High Power from the Alessi rig under his jeans jacket, the hammer already cocked, his right thumb wiping down the safety. The pistol bucked once, then once more, in his right hand as he fired into the mass of KGB men storming toward the ditch. The .44 Magnum went off beside him and three men fell—

two by Frost and one by O'Hara as Frost judged it.

Frost glanced to his right—Jessica Pace wasn't even looking toward the battle; her eyes had a faraway look to them. The Walther was in her hand, the hammer cocked, her right first finger stroking the trigger so gently the gun wasn't discharging.

"What the hell are you doing?" Frost snapped, clamping his hand over the gun and working the safety. The girl glared up at him.

Frost said nothing. Having dropped the pistol in her lap, he swung the muzzle of the KG-9 over the top of the ditch and fired strings of two-round bursts. The KGB men had fallen back, the burning wreckage of the airplane between their positions and to Frost's far right.

"Well—what d'ya think?" O'Hara rasped through gritted teeth.

Frost, looking back over the lip of the ditch, reloaded the KG-9 magazines by feel and answered, "I think we're in trouble, O'Hara. I don't know how you feel about—just call it a gut reaction I've got."

"Smart ass!"

"How's my neck look?" Frost asked, ignoring O'Hara.

"Terrific," O'Hara snarled. "If ya' like gunshot wounds. You'll live. I had worse; so've you."

Frost rubbed at his neck, feeling the blood trickling more slowly there, then nodded silently in agreement.

"I got this all figured," O'Hara muttered.

Frost looked at him. "What?"

"This—this whole deal how we get the young lady

out o' this."

Frost looked at Jessica Pace on his right, her eyes staring up over the lip of the ditch now.

"Just how do we do that—or is that something they only teach you in G-man school?"

"Shut up, will ya—you're about to have a brilliant plan whipped on ya—and you make light of it. Boy, what a—"

There was a long burst of automatic-weapons fire. "They're comin' again," O'Hara snapped.

"Like they say in the western movies—I'm runnin' out of ammo. I got half a load or so in the Browning, four extra magazines and about half a stick in the KG-9. I figure you've got two or three speedloaders left and some loose spares, right?"

"Two speedloaders exactly," O'Hara snorted, "and maybe a dozen loose rounds in my pockets—then five rounds and a speedloader for the Model 60," he added.

"Wonderful—this assault!" Frost fired two more rounds, taking his time, nailing a KGB man with an M-16 coming at them in a zig-zag run, ". . . and one more and we're out."

"Yeah—well—I got that figured, too, see," O'Hara said. "You get the woman to leave me her peashooter there so I can make 'em think there's more than one of us here. Then you take her around behind that stand of trees where the airplane crashed and steal one of the Ruskie's cars and boogie out of here—I'll link up with ya' later."

Frost fired a two-round burst; a chunky-looking KGB man went down as he crossed from one side of the clearing separating them to the other. Frost turned around and looked at O'Hara. "You're signing your own death warrant, O'Hara."

"Baloney—that's crazy talk. Once they see you guys pull away in the car, they'll be after you—I'm givin' myself a break, can't ya see that?"

"Bullshit," Frost said quietly. Frost looked at the girl, then back at O'Hara. "You don't have to do it—she'll stand a better chance of getting by the CIA and FBI people with you."

"Look—we don't have time for all this. I'm a federal officer—let's say I'm deputizin' you. Now do what I tell ya to."

"What?" Frost asked, swapping two shots over the lip of the ditch and bringing down another KGB man. Two more cars had pulled up, dumping out another dozen men. "You gonna arrest me?"

"Yeah—maybe." O'Hara smiled.

Frost looked back at the girl. "Give your gun to O'Hara, Jessica. We're cuttin' out—you and me."

Frost started to move but before he could twist around toward her, he realized it was too late. At the edge of his peripheral vision, he could see O'Hara's chest almost thumping as the slugs tore into it. O'Hara's left arm spouting blood, O'Hara falling back against the rocks at the side of the drainage ditch. Frost reached out for the gun in Jessica Pace's right hand, reached for it as he almost felt it going off. In slow motion he saw the action working back as he felt the explosion in his head, saw the colors in front of his eye . . . his head exploded; he felt, sensed, almost as if he were standing there watching it—until the blackness flooded across his eye. . .

Chapter Fifteen

Frost opened his eye. He decided it was the ultimate insult. Here he was, obviously dead, and there was O'Hara—dead, too—still rattling on and complaining. Frost listened to the words. ". . . among the livin' there, sport."

"Living?"

"Yeah— what's—"

"You're dead—I saw you take three rounds in the chest."

"God bless the folks at Second Chance—first thing I do when I get dressed in the morning is put on the old vest, ya know? Looks and feels just like a good old American T-shirt, stops them bullets just great. 'Cept when she shot me in the arm here.'' O'Hara gestured toward his left arm in a sling, the arm bandaged around the bicep.

"What are you talkin' about?" Frost groaned. His head ached, his mouth felt as though he'd smoked six cartons of cigarettes in a row.

"She shot me, I stumbled back—hit the old noggin on a rock and the lights went out—just as she shot you."

"She shot me in the head," Frost stammered.

"Yeah—good thing for you she didn't aim for a vital area—ha!"

"Oh, shut up." Frost groaned. He started to move his head but felt as though he were going to throw up.

"You must've zigged when she zagged—creased your skull good. Another quarter of an inch and I'da got nailed with a bill for flowers for your funeral, Frost. You realize what flowers cost?"

"O'Hara—" Frost started to push himself up on the bed; his head ached as though someone were hitting him there with a rifle butt. He saw the floaters—red and some other color he couldn't identify—washing in front of his eyes.

He thought he heard O'Hara—still rattling on—shout, "Hey—get the croaker in here!"

Frost opened his eye. It hadn't been a nightmare. O'Hara was sitting on the end of the bed, left arm still in a sling, a crazy smile on his face. "You're up, huh! Good—like I was tellin' ya, the Pace dame—"

"How long have I been out?" Frost asked, his voice sounding tired and weak to him.

"Two hours or so. Try not to pass out this time, Frost—I need ya. I'll get the guys."

"What guys?" Frost started to ask, but O'Hara was already up, moving toward the door and opening it. There was a loud whistle—like someone calling a taxicab—and then Frost heard O'Hara muttering something that sounded like, "Yeah—sorry, nurse—yeah—I know there's people sleepin'—right, gotcha, sweetheart."

Frost tried moving his head, to turn away from the door. "What guys?" he muttered.

He couldn't move his head, so he looked at the doorway. There was O'Hara again, and with him six men, one of them wearing a police uniform.

"Gentlemen—this is Capt. Hank Frost—my old buddy from up in Canada there where we did that number on those terrorists."

"Captain Frost." One of the older men smiled, extending his right hand. Frost feebly reached out his right hand and shook with the man.

"Frost," another man muttered; the rest of them just grunted things Frost couldn't understand.

"Now—gotta get this Jessica Pace thing nailed down, huh?"

Frost moved his head—slightly, slowly—and looked at O'Hara. "Mike," he said, using O'Hara's first name for only the second time in his life, "what the hell is going on?"

"Better tell him, O'Hara," the older man Frost had shaken hands with said, his voice oozing authority.

"Yes, sir," O'Hara said. Then O'Hara turned toward Frost. "See—I don't know exactly what happened. Got the bump on my head, here." O'Hara rubbed the back of his skull dramatically. "The Pace dame evidently went all the way in the bonkers bureau and decided to smoke us both. Did such a convincing job of it, the KGB guys must've let us alone. They wanted her to begin with—at least we think so."

"What are you talking about?" Frost asked, feeling sick to his stomach. "Give me a cigarette, somebody."

Suddenly Frost felt as if he were in the center of a consumer taste test. Five packs of cigarettes were extended to him and Frost—not seeing his own brand—grabbed a Pall Mall. Somebody—he thought it was the uniformed policeman—lit it for him. Frost inhaled the smoke, hard, and, his head starting to reel, fell back against the pillow.

He shook his head, the motion making his head ache again, but he dragged on the cigarette once more. His eye focused on the man in the police uniform. He seemed awfully old for a uniformed policeman, Frost thought. Then he noticed the tailoring of the uniform, the brass on the epaulets.

"Thanks, there, commissioner," O'Hara snapped.

Frost looked at O'Hara, then asked, "Commissioner?"

"Yeah, Frost." O'Hara smiled. "This is Commissioner Bohen, with the police. This is Assistant Bureau Director—"

"Bureau?"

"Yeah—FBI—you know. Assistant Director Craigin; this is CIA Assistant Deputy Director Morris Filtchner; this is—"

"Wait—what's goin'?"

"Maybe I'd better explain." Frost turned his head, slowly. It was the man from the FBI, the one O'Hara had identified as a deputy director or assistant something. Frost couldn't remember, but he remembered the man's name was Craigin. "See—it's clear Jessica Pace shot you and Special Agent O'Hara, Captain Frost. But why is what we're uncertain of at this juncture."

"I don't—" Frost began, then felt his voice drifting off, his throat tightening.

"Don't try to talk—just listen. It's important that you do. First of all," Craigin said, clearing his throat as if preparing for a long speech, "we cleared up all the charges against you. Regardless of what Miss Pace is up to, it's clear you and your superior, Mr. Deacon, were acting with the best of motives—and I am personally seeing to it that Special Agent O'Hara gets a commendation for his part in this thing. But be that as it may," Frost hated the expression, "we have a problem, and only you and Mr. O'Hara can assist us in the resolution of this difficulty."

"I don't—"

"You will—at least as well as we understand it, Captain Frost. The problem, simply put is that we don't know who Jessica Pace really is. From what Special Agent O'Hara has told us, it seems she was under a great deal of mental strain, something like combat fatigue. That could have been genuine, or just an act she put on to throw you both off. Consider the possibilities."

Frost started searching for an ashtray, thinking the man named Craigin sounded as though he were selling him a used car with a built-in vacuum cleaner and a set of encyclopedias in the trunk. He found the ashtray when someone put it in front of him.

"We know that there really *is* a Jessica Pace—or at least was. That she was supposed to have been substituted for a KGB agent to whom she was nearly identical physically. But, was the Jessica Pace you were bodyguarding the real Jessica Pace, or was she Irena Pavarova?"

"I don't follow you at all," Frost told Craigin, shaking his head, searching out another cigarette—this time a Chesterfield.

"It's simple, sport," O'Hara began. "The only thing that makes sense in this thing is the facts. I woke up out there, my gun full of mud and crap, my arm bleedin' like it was goin' out of style and you with a head wound that looked like somethin' out of an old first-aid film. You were in shock, too. I found myself the road, tried hailin' down a ride, finally got a trucker to stop when I waved my badge at him. I used his CB to call home, got the ambulance out there—the whole nine yards. Anyway, she shot you and she shot me. We know that. Looked as if she was crackin' up—I don't think it was an act. Those KGB guys took off either after her or with her. We don't know. Calvin Plummer is still so trusted by the President that Mr. Craigin here couldn't get the president even to admit to the meeting—but our private sources say it's scheduled. So—so, we got this dame who's either a fruitcake or an assassin. And maybe she's got this list—"

"If she has, we can't avoid the meeting because the information is so important it's got to be revealed. And we must see that she remains unharmed," Craigin said solemnly.

"But if she isn't Jessica Pace, or if there's somethin' else screwy goin' on, we gotta stop her," O'Hara said through his teeth.

"The possibilities are endless, aren't they?" Frost said, his voice sounding tired to him.

"I concur," the man introduced as Filtchner said. Frost seemed to remember the man was supposed to be with the CIA.

"I decided to gamble and call in the good guys—the ones I knew were the good guys, Frost. Had to," O'Hara said, his voice oddly serious-sounding.

Frost tried to nod, then grunted something instead. "What, ahh—"

"It must be determined," Craigin said, "just who the young lady in question is—first and foremost. Is she Jessica Pace? Is she Irena Pavarova and Jessica never replaced her at all? Did Irena perhaps have a twin sister and the Russians got wise to Jessica Pace and took her out of the picture and replaced her with a third look-alike? Basically, can we trust Calvin Plummer to bring this girl in contact with the President of the United States. What will she do? And if she is Jessica Pace, is she still sane enough to be relied upon? All questions that need answers—and you and Mr. O'Hara have to get them."

Frost started to laugh—then stopped. Nobody else was laughing.

"We have men—joint teams to keep an eye on each other, really," Filtchner said. "They have Miss Pace or whoever she is under a sort of loose surveillance."

"What he's tryin' to say is they know approximately where she is, but nobody's seen her," O'Hara snapped.

"You—" Filtchner sighed. "You are right—but we're working to correct that. We've got surveillance teams at all the airports, railway stations, bus depots—everywhere. And we're also picking up every KGB man we can find—for everything from bad visas to overdue parking tickets. We're trying to get her safely into the Washington area, but keep her from getting to the President—until we know. And that is what you and O'Hara are supposed to find out about."

"How can—" Frost let the question hang, gesturing across his body in the hospital bed.

"Doctors say you can be up and around tomorrow if it's important enough. May have some bad headaches, but we can get you a prescription for that. O'Hara's arm doesn't discount him either. You are the two men in whom we can place ultimate trust. You both had ample opportunity to kill Jessica Pace and neither of you did. You can't be on her list, Captain Frost—you're not *in* FBI or CIA. Obviously O'Hara isn't or he would have killed you both or died trying. We have no one else we can send."

"Send where?" Frost asked Craigin.

"This little place Plummer has in the Smoky Mountains." O'Hara smiled. "Kind of a combination safe house, training area, and retreat. He's supposed to have Irena Pavarova there.''

"What?"

"When Jessica Pace was supposedly substituted for Irena Pavarova—" Filtchner said. "Well, it was decided by all concerned that it was best to keep the real woman on ice—just in case she was ever needed for a trade, etc. Plummer's had her there. It's not really a prison—she's free to move around, write, read, do what she wants as long as she doesn't try to escape the grounds. There was a rumor that she'd tried once and Plummer's people got her back.''

"We gotta go see who he's got there—Jessica or Irena,'' O'Hara said finally.

"We're all crazy,'' Frost said. "I can barely lift my head up and tomorrow I'm supposed to penetrate a tight-security prison in the Smokies and find a woman who looks just like the woman who shot me. Then what do we do—ask her a bunch of questions? How do we know if it's really Jessica or Irena?

"And what do we do when we find out who's who?''

"If it's Irena, Frost,'' O'Hara said, "we pat her on the fannie and give her back to Plummer. If it's Jessica—well,'' and O'Hara paused.

"If it's Jessica,'' Filtchner said, "either you and O'Hara kill Plummer or we do—and then we stop Irena or whoever she is from assassinating the President of the United States.''

"And what if we can't determine?'' Frost asked.

O'Hara smiled. "We improvise.''

Frost started to say something, but instead he dragged on the Chesterfield. Improvise, he thought—that meant kill everybody, just in case.

Chapter Sixteen

The doctor having given him a shaky approval for discharge, Frost had cleaned his own Browning High Power and the Interdynamics KG-9 before leaving the hospital that morning. Fresh ammo, supplied with his favorite brand by the "task force" O'Hara had put together, filled the magazines of his guns and all the spares; two boxes more were in his pack. There was a borrowed M-16 as well with a half-dozen thirty-round magazines and a GI-issue bayonet. O'Hara had improvised a little additional armament as well, Frost thought. In addition to the FBI man's habitual arsenal there was a sawed-off double-barreled shotgun of indeterminate make, the butt stock all but gone, and all that remained a much taped-over pistol grip with a lanyard loop on it. This rabbit-eared double hung on a sling under O'Hara's leather jacket by the lanyard loop, hammers down. Frost wondered secretly if it had come from some museum or was improvised for the occasion.

Frost checked the black-faced Rolex Oyster Perpetual Submariner on his wrist—it was time for another pain pill for the ache in his head. He popped the pill, hoping it would have more effect than the last one, then followed it up with a swig of warm-tasting water from the GI-issue plastic canteen on his pistol belt. Pistol belt, he thought. His pistol was in his shoulder rig, but the name "pistol belt" seemed somehow to fall off the tongue better than any other.

"How's the arm?" Frost shouted over the whirring rotor blades.

"Just perfect—I think I'll keep it bandaged forever like this," O'Hara snapped.

"How can you take that shoulder rig—with the arm, I mean?" Frost shouted again.

"It's cheaper than buyin' a belt holster—anyway, just my arm, not my shoulder. How's your head?"

Frost felt the bandage taped to his right temple. "Lousy."

"Good for ya'," the FBI man shouted back. "Seems whenever we work together we get ourselves shot up—glad we don't do it too often." O'Hara laughed.

"Me too—I couldn't take it." Frost laughed.

There was little talking after that; Frost gave a final check to the M-16—the selector lever was a little stiff but functional—and O'Hara, to Frost's distraction, checked the action of the sawed-off twelve-gauge. There was no plan, really, but to get out of the helicopter drop zone as fast as possible and get as close to Plummer's sanctuary as they could before they started bumping heads and generally alerting Plummer's elite guard that they were around and interested in interviewing the woman held there.

Frost still wondered what they would ask Irena Pavarova/Jessica Pace to determine her real identity. Frost knew about the operation to fake a broken leg, about the operations on Jessica Pace's fingertips to change her prints, about all of the things in Jessica's and Irena's background—O'Hara had read them to him the previous night because Frost's head ached too much to read the files himself. But nothing in the files gave Frost any indication of how to tell one girl from the other. It was logical to assume that though Jessica would know everything about Irena, Irena would know little or nothing about Jessica. Perhaps they could take the tack of questioning the woman in Plummer's hideaway about the background of Jessica Pace. If she knew too much, it was obviously Jessica—unless Plummer was truly devious and for some reason had fed Irena that information.

Frost's head ached more when he thought about it. He glanced at the Rolex again. Bess . . .

Twenty minutes remained before the drop zone would come up. Frost decided to try to sleep.

Perhaps it would help the pill take effect. . . .

He'd opened his eye five minutes before the drop when O'Hara shook him.

As Frost crouched now behind an outcropping of green lichen-covered rock, staring up toward the villalike walled house above him, he decided he'd have been happier if O'Hara had just let him go on sleeping. The pain in his head had started to subside shortly after the drop and now it was starting to come back. The one-eyed man decided it was possibly psychosomatic—the pain in his head was a way of telling himself that if he went up to the walled house held by Calvin Plummer's men he could get killed. Stay back instead, nurse your wounds. He shook his head, making the pain worse. Staying back was something Frost had never been able to do, and he didn't really wish that it had ever been any different.

Frost glanced over to O'Hara; charging along up the rocks and ravines toward the top of the mountains had obviously been hard on the man. Frost had seen some of the best men get themselves so weary fighting a wound that their reaction time had gone bad; they'd gotten careless—there was a whole catalog of things that could cause someone to do something stupid and get killed. Frost knew because he had worked himself through that catalog and come close to death too often. Looking at O'Hara he realized that this loud-mouthed FBI man was one of the few real friends he had—and he had no desire to lose him.

"Mike?" Frost found himself using O'Hara's first

name again.

"Yeah!" The weariness was more in O'Hara's voice and in his eyes than in the way he moved or behaved. Frost realized that O'Hara was well aware of the problem his wound was causing him, but trying to hide it. It wasn't working.

"I'm going in by myself."

"Bullshit—I'm goin' with ya to keep ya out of—".

Frost punched O'Hara lightly on the left arm. The FBI man's eyes went tight with apparent pain, his right hand almost involuntarily moved up to protect the wound. "What happens when somebody slugs you there, or you bump into a rock or a doorknob, O'Hara? What if we get into a good run?"

"What are ya talkin' a—"

"You've got one choice, O'Hara," Frost rasped, feeling his teeth clench, his lips drawn back over them. "You try to stop me, the only way you can do it is to use a gun. You can't take me in a fight the way you are with that arm. You use a gun and they hear you and the whole deal is blown. You try taggin' after me, and I don't go in—period. Now what's it gonna be?"

"You son of a—"

Frost cut him off again. "Now sometimes even a guy like me gets pissed, O'Hara. I just lost my woman—some damned terrorists killed her, blew her up so bad I didn't even have a body to bury. And I don't give a damn what you think, because I'm not about to lose my best friend—now I'm goin'. Try to stop me if you want to."

Frost pushed himself to his feet, his head aching again, the M-16 slung under his right arm.

Chapter Seventeen

Frost had memorized the map of the compound, comforted by the fact that there was apparently no electronic security outside it. In an area with a large deer population, stray dogs, perhaps even an occasional bear, an intruder-alert system on the outside of the walls would have been of no benefit since it would have been constantly going off and eventually would have been generally ignored.

And it really wasn't necessary, Frost decided. There were the signs around the area that read U.S. GOVERNMENT INSTALLATION—PRIVATE PROPERTY—TRESPASSERS WILL BE PROSECUTED—DO NOT

ENTER—NO UNAUTHORIZED TRAFFIC BEYOND THIS POINT. Frost had never seen so many signs meaning one thing—keep out. And the signs were backed up, he realized. Though no guns were present, he had already spotted two men on the wall surrounding the house. Frost wondered what some staid Tennessee citizen might have thought—an armed camp, a prison, a spy school really, set like a rusty tin can in the middle of the incredibly beautiful Smoky Mountains.

Frost started to push himself up from where he crouched behind some low rocks, but glanced up, and instead flattened himself against the ground, dragging the M-16 with him as he rolled across the rocky soil into a stand of pines. There was an unmistakable sound in the air, the whirring of rotor blades. Frost looked up, his eye squinted against the sun. A shiver ran down his spine—as the helicopter dipped low over him, going over the wall, he noticed the markings. The shiver came from one peculiar marking in particular. The seal of the President of the United States.

"The meeting," the one-eyed man rasped to himself. The meeting between Jessica Pace or whoever she was was taking place already—here—now. Frost kept below the concealment of the pine boughs as the chopper sped across his line of sight, disappearing over the wall.

His mind raced. "O'Hara!" Frost pushed to his feet, the attention of the guards on the wall momentarily turned toward its interior perimeter, he noticed, as he broke cover and ran, back down the mountainside. "O'Hara!" the one-eyed man rasped.

Frost ran hard, his lungs already burning with the exertion, the pain in his head throbbed. "Stupid!" he rasped to himself, his breath coming in short gasps. He saw it all. Plummer had been the set-up all along, he realized. The whole thing with Jessica Pace—whoever she was—was to get the President of the United States moved from point A to point B. If there was a list, if Jessica Pace was a good agent with a bad case of battle fatigue or if she was really a Russian—it was all one red herring piled on top of another. The entire purpose of the thing had been to get the President of the United States into Plummer's compound—like the spider inviting the fly into his parlor.

Frost jumped a low pile of rocks, and started to trip, his left ankle buckling, but caught himself. Perhaps he should have stormed the compound by himself, Frost thought, picking himself up, keeping on running. Perhaps a wild shot toward the presidential helicopter would have scared the President off, prevented what Frost knew was about to happen. Was it already happening?

Frost rounded the edge of a stand of cedar trees—beautiful, he thought almost absently—and tripped over O'Hara.

"What the—!"

"O'Hara—that helicopter—you see it?" Frost asked, gasping for breath.

"Yeah—big deal. Probably choppers comin' in and out of there all day. So?"

Frost's hands were on O'Hara's shoulders. He realized it when he saw the pain in O'Hara's eyes. "Mike—that was the presidential chopper—Air

Force One with the President aboard. It's the meeting—here, now!''

"Holy shit!"

"Ditto—come on."

Frost started to his feet, then turned, O'Hara grabbing him by the arm. "Why'd you—"

"Hell—I don't know." Frost laughed, then started running. Frost slowed after the first hundred yards or so, wheeling, seeing O'Hara trying to keep up. It reminded him of something. Frost risked the shout, "Gonna change your name to Peter?" Then, laughing, Frost rasped, "Come on O'Hara!"

The FBI man, his face lined with pain, his left arm clamped tight against his body in the sling, shouted back, "Very funny—ha! See—I'm—I'm laughing, already!"

Frost swung the M-16 off his right shoulder and into a high port, still running, slowing again, letting O'Hara catch up. There was only one way for it, Frost realized. Storm into the compound, alerting the secret-service men guarding the President. Maybe that way Plummer wouldn't be able to get the job done.

Frost's heart sank—he heard shots from up ahead, from the compound. His lungs ached. As he ran, the one-eyed man screamed, "No—No!"

The wall was a hundred yards ahead and on the wall Frost could see one of the two guards he'd seen earlier, an M-16 in his hands, but turned away toward the inside of the compound, the gun firing. Frost threw himself to the ground, hauled the butt of his own M-16 to his right shoulder, then cursed the iron sights. The selector set to full auto, he squeezed the trigger. He could see the rock of the wall chipping, see the guard with the M-16 starting to turn, the muzzle spouting flame. Frost kept firing, the guard started to wheel in a full circle, his M-16 still firing as the man toppled over the wall. Frost pushed himself to his feet. Firing out the thirty-round magazine as he raced toward the wall, Frost began shouting, screaming, "Surrender Plummer—we've got you surrounded!" Frost heard a boom from behind him, half-spun around, to see O'Hara, the big six-inch Model 29 in his right hand. Frost looked back to the wall, then down by the main gate—it was opening, three men raced through it into the open, one of them falling back, hands clasping his chest.

Frost rammed the fresh stick into the M-16, then sprayed the 5.56-mm death pills toward the open gate, cutting down the remaining two men there, then starting to run again. He could hear the whirring of rotor blades, the sound seemed to grow in intensity as he stormed toward the gates. Frost hit the ground, the M-16 snaking out ahead of him, firing, a half-dozen men charging toward him. Frost caught the first man, then the second, then felt something tearing across his back—pain! He rolled, firing, killing a burly man charging at him with an M-16. Frost started to his feet, his back burning. He glanced down at the sandy ground of the compound—it was dark red with blood where he'd lain.

Frost fired a three-round burst, then another and another—there were four more men still coming at him. One went down, then another. Frost's left shoulder felt as if it were being torn away from him;

he wheeled on his heels, started to stumble. The sandy ground slammed up toward him. He kept firing, one three-round burst cutting into the two men still running for him, the nearer man's face bursting at the nose in a massive flower of blood, the second man doubling over. Behind them, Frost could see the presidential helicopter, three men on the ground near it, firing toward two men in three-piece business suits holding Uzis. Frost started to his feet, then fell back. The roaring sound seeming to slap him down physically; his body shuddered, the fireball of yellow, orange, and black so bright it almost blinded him as he hit the ground.

He could smell the oil burning, hear the crackling sounds, the smaller secondary explosions. He could see the black bones of the chopper, flames licking from them.

But there was still shooting from the far end of the compound. "He's alive!" Frost felt the words more than heard them as they fell from his lips. He pushed himself up on his hands and knees, changing sticks in the M-16, firing toward Plummer's men at the far side of the compound. He could see Plummer there—he recognized the tall, white-haired man from a photograph shown him that morning. And beside Plummer, crouched behind an automobile, was Jessica Pace—or perhaps Irena Pavarova. Both of them held automatic weapons. Far beyond them, Frost could hear the rattle of light-caliber gunfire, automatic weapons—Uzi submachine guns, the kind carried by the secret service.

There were another half-dozen men storming toward him now. Frost, having forced himself to his feet, the M-16 held low at his right hip in an assault position, could no longer run. He just walked and fired. He shot the nearest man, who tumbled like a bowling pin, spinning first, and rolling to the sandy ground.

Again there was the booming sound of O'Hara's 29. A second man went down. Frost kept firing.

"God!" Frost screamed, doubling over, feeling the slugs hammering into his guts as he toppled forward, his M-16 on full auto chewing into the ground.

He heard the boom of O'Hara's .44 again as he looked up to see another of the men belonging to Plummer hit the ground.

"It's all right, sport!" Frost heard the familiar voice grunting. "Come on—up!"

Frost's left arm moved—he didn't know if he moved it himself or not. He looked to his left, saw O'Hara, then felt his left arm burning and saw the blood on it. "Gotta do it this way—hold on to me. Can't do it with the left hand!"

Frost glanced toward O'Hara. The sling on O'Hara's arm was gone; the sawed-off shotgun was in his left hand, braced against O'Hara's side. Frost had the M-16, the muzzle coming up.

There was gunfire everywhere, deafeningly loud. He couldn't think. "O'Hara—change sticks for me."

"Gotcha!"

More gunfire—Frost's left leg started to buckle. The M-16 wasn't in his hands anymore. He snatched the Browning High Power from under his jeans jacket; his thumb cocked the hammer, and he pumped the trigger. One round, then another, then another, and another.

The nearest of Plummer's men spun out and went down.

"Here, Frost!"

Frost jammed the High Power into his belt, his right fist—there was blood dripping down his wrist—wrapping around the pistol grip of the M-16. He fired a test burst into the ground a few yards ahead of him, then muttered, "All right!"

There was a booming noise as Frost, supported against O'Hara's right shoulder, started slowly forward. He glanced toward O'Hara—the sawed-off twelve-gauge was coming down and out a whiplash like recoil. Ahead of them, three men were rolling on the ground. One of them started to his feet. Frost pumped a three-round burst into the man with the M-16.

"O.K.!" O'Hara was moving, and Frost, leaning on him again, was moving with him.

The light automatic fire—the Uzis—was rattling on; the heavier, somehow different-sound stacatto of the M-16s almost drowned it out.

Frost's left leg was burning. His back was making him scream. He could hear himself as he stumbled forward beside O'Hara.

Frost could see Plummer and the red-haired woman beside him; see them turning toward himself and O'Hara. Plummer was shouting something. "Get the President now—move in!"

Frost fired the M-16 at the nearest targets of opportunity. There were two dozen men storming across the courtyard, but not toward him and O'Hara.

"Let's fix that, Mike," Frost snarled.

O'Hara stopped and Frost's left arm snaked off the FBI man's shoulders.

It was the kind of gunfight, Frost thought almost absently, that supposedly never took place. Two men, against ten times that many—both men knowing they were going to die and not caring, maybe because of the electricity of insanity that seemed to flow across the ground in such a way that Frost could almost feel it. Death—he could feel it welling up within him.

The M-16 was in his right hand, the Browning High Power in his left. His left leg didn't work well and it was stiff as he started walking again, his steps short so he wouldn't stumble.

O'Hara was beside him. Their eyes met a moment. The sawed-off shotgun was in O'Hara's left hand, the Model 29 in his right.

O'Hara was walking too. For the first time, Frost noticed a large, wet-looking red spot on O'Hara's right side.

"I'd say it's been nice knowin' ya, but I don't wanna kick off with a lie in my throat." O'Hara laughed, shouting over the roar of the gunfire.

Frost heard himself laughing as he walked forward, heard—felt—his guns firing into the two dozen men storming toward the President of the United States and his few remaining secret-service guards.

Plummer's men were going down. Frost felt slugs tearing into him, dropped to his knees, then kept going forward, crawling. He lost track of the booming sounds of O'Hara's guns, of the men belonging to

Plummer who were dying.

Frost, using the empty M-16 as a crutch, pushed himself back to his feet, the Browning empty, too, now and jammed into his belt, the KG-9 swinging out on its sling from under his left arm, the pistol grip coming into his left hand. His right hand wasn't working well, the fingers not responding to him.

He started firing again, glancing to his left. He knew now why he no longer heard the booming sounds of O'Hara's guns—the icy-eyed FBI man was face down in the dirt, a red stain spreading under him, the big Model 29 still in his right fist.

"Bastards!" Frost was screaming, his throat aching as he lurched forward, the KG-9 spitting death into the wall of Plummer's men, now turned toward him. He could hear the rattling of the Uzis, coming closer—were the secret-service men trying to get the President out? Was the President still—"Aagh!" Frost stumbled forward, his mouth open and suddenly filled with sand. He coughed once, blood speckling the sand. He shoved the KG-9 ahead of him, ready to fire.

But there was no gunfire.

He looked up—Calvin Plummer, clad in black slacks, a black turtleneck shirt, and sixty-five-dollar shoes, Frost thought. There was a submachine gun in his hands. And beside him was a woman. She wore blue jeans, track shoes, and a faded blue T-shirt. There was a Walther PPK in her hands.

"Jessica." Frost coughed.

He tried to raise the KG-9. There was a shot. He saw Plummer's eyes widening, saw the red-haired woman wheeling around, heard the gun in her hands firing, felt the hot brass as it spit into his cheek. More pistol shots. Frost closed his eye.

"Holy—"

It was Jessica Pace, and Jessica Pace again. The two of them—identical down to the track shoes—were walking toward each other across the courtyard, their pistols firing, the pistols, too, identical. "Dreaming—nightmare," Frost rasped, coughing up more blood.

Calvin Plummer was stumbling across the courtyard. Frost twisted on the ground, coughing again, edging the KG-9 through the dust. He twitched his left hand, the trigger responding, the assault pistol firing once, then falling from Frost's hand. Calvin Plummer fell over, dead. Frost knew the man was dead—the shot had hit Plummer square in the back of the neck over the spine.

There were two more shots and Frost turned his head to see.

The two women—the two identical women—were down on the dirt, unmoving. "Killed each—each other." He coughed. He thought how funny it was—that good and bad sometimes mixed so much you could no longer tell them apart. He felt sorry, too—too bad he was dying and he wouldn't get to write that down. As he closed his eye, he caught sight of the Rolex watch on his left wrist, the second hand sweeping around. He wondered how long it would go on moving like that, after— "Bess." The one-eyed man coughed as he closed his one eye.

Chapter Eighteen

There was no funeral. Jessica Pace had long ago been declared legally dead anyway, before ever undertaking Plummer's assignment. And the way the two women had fallen, though it was clear one was the real Jessica and one was Irena Pavarova, no one was certain which of the two women had been fighting beside Plummer in the abortive attempt to murder the President of the United States and make it appear to be a plot of the U.S. intelligence community to take over the country. And no one was able to tell which of the two women had been with Frost and O'Hara, had talked about the list, perhaps believed in the validity of the names there enough to die for it. The list had been contrived by

Plummer as an excuse to bring Jessica—if it had been Jessica—out of the Soviet Union as the catalyst for his plan to get the President to the mountain hideaway where Plummer planned to murder him.

The latter was clear from Plummer's notes, found in a hidden safe in the house. Beyond that, why Plummer had wanted the President dead, whether he had worked for the Russians or some private group of conspirators, was not certain. Plummer had died and taken the information with him.

Commendations for the gallant sacrifices of Frost and O'Hara had been private and unofficial. Three secret-service men had died—officially labeled a helicopter crash during a training exercise. The attack—nearly successful—on the life of the President had officially never taken place.

Whether the real Jessica Pace had been a tragic, nerves-worn-raw girl obsessed with completing a mission, a brilliant actress, or a prisoner of the Plummer compound was never established.

"Here—I'll buy ya a beer," O'Hara said.

Frost looked up from the small table in the back of the restaurant, the familiarly abrasive voice interrupting his thoughts. "O'Hara—I heard you were gettin' out."

Frost noticed the cane. He'd had one, too, until a few days before. The back wound still hurt when he moved too fast. O'Hara started to sit down, stretching out his bad left leg. It was Frost's left leg that had gotten it, too. O'Hara's eyes got glassy hard as he bent into the seat. The belly wound? Frost wondered.

"I got ya a present."

"What—you? Those turkeys of Plummer's couldn't

even knock you off for me—what a bunch of—"

"Yeah—crumb-bums, I know. Well . . . I wasn't too pleased when I heard you were in the same hospital. When I woke up I thought I was rid of ya for good there."

"Can't win 'em all." Frost smiled, lighting a Camel in the blue-yellow flame of his Zippo. Eight weeks of his life were gone, more than that when he counted the time since he'd left the hospital, and the time spent in the cross-country ride with Jessica or Irena—whoever it had been. That was the part that most bothered him—who had he made love to, screamed at, cursed, and protected? Why had she shot him?

"Ya don't wanna see your gift?"

O'Hara had been nine weeks in the hospital and Frost had visited him twice. The meeting at the restaurant wasn't an accident. The two men had agreed upon it a week earlier when Frost had visited O'Hara just before O'Hara's discharge.

Frost was tired of Washington. His strength was returning and he was planning to make arrangements to get back to Europe within the week—after one more appointment with the doctors on the back wound.

"So—what's the gift?"

"You still plannin' on trackin' down the guys that blew up that London department store?"

Frost looked down at the second hand of the Rolex on his wrist and nodded, dragging heavily on the cigarette between his lips.

"Figured you were. I got the bureau—unofficially—to put a few screws into some of their ties with European police agencies. Got you somethin'."

"A lead on who—"

"Maybe it's somethin' that'll drive you crazy, maybe it'll make you kill yourself, maybe it means somethin' good. I hope it means somethin' good for ya—here."

"What—?"

O'Hara was fishing into his pocket. He set down on the table a worn velvet ring box.

"I lost it, I guess." Frost smiled, picking it up, turning it over in his hand.

"Open it up, Hank—open it."

Frost opened it, the cigarette dropping from his lips. The diamond glinted at him in the overhead lighting, the diamond set into the mouth of a golden tiger, in the braided chain band he'd had sized down to fit Bess's finger—the diamond that she'd worn when the terrorist bomb had gone off in the department store in London.

Frost looked up at O'Hara. His throat was tight. He wanted to ask something.

"West German police picked it up on a terrorist named Kolner—but before you ask, the guy had it on a chain around his neck when the cops shot him during a robbery."

"But if he had the ring and she was—"

"Yeah, I know," the icy-eyed FBI man said, his teeth clenched tight together. "Maybe Bess is alive out there."

Frost stared down at the diamond in the mouth of the tiger, turning it over in his hands. After a long minute he couldn't see it too well with his one good eye—he had the same problem sometimes at night when he couldn't sleep. "Bess," Frost whispered.